Motherhood

Lindsey Williams

Cover layout and design by Lindsey Williams

Copyright © 2015 Lindsey Williams
All rights reserved. No part of this publication may be reproduced, distributed, or transmitted in any form or by any means, or stored in a database or retrieval system, without the prior written permission of the publisher.

First Edition: 2015

The characters and events in this book are fictitious. The events depicted may be disturbing to some and reading is not recommended for those under the age of 18. Any similarities to real persons, living or dead, is coincidental and not intended by the author. Any use of trademarked names, brands or businesses is acknowledged as the respective property of their owner/s and is used for purely fictional purposes not meant to depict specific places, events or product placement.

CHAPTER ONE

Jess Richards woke with a start and bolted upright. Or tried to anyway. She slid sideways about halfway up and found herself in a brief free-fall, after which she landed on her side with a grunt.

She lay stunned on the cold, hard floor with her eyes squeezed shut, afraid to open them. Because when she did, it would confirm what she *thought* she'd seen as she fell.

After delaying the inevitable as long as possible, she reluctantly opened her eyes and sat up with a groan, rubbing her now throbbing shoulder.

The tiny hairs on the back of her neck stood at attention as she registered her surroundings. A shiver wracked her body from the sensation and her pulse raced as adrenaline flooded her system.

"What the ever living hell is going on here?" she asked of no one in particular. Her voice echoed oddly in the room.

She looked around to discover she was indeed alone. Which was not in itself unusual as she lived alone in her apartment. But she also wasn't *in* her apartment.

"Oh my god. Where am I?" she said, with mounting dread.

The room was about ten feet by ten at her guess, with steel walls and a steel floor and ceiling. It had no obvious door and nothing in it except for her and a steel gurney.

A fucking gurney? she thought. *Why is there so much steel in this room? And where's the door?*

The last thing she remembered was crashing into bed after her usual shift at Macy's and some drinks with a few of her girlfriends.

Now she was inside a goddamned steel box. In her pajamas. She stared down at her sky blue lounge pants, her mind unwilling to process the information it had been given.

After a long moment of empty incomprehension, the fragments clicked into place.

I've been kidnapped.

Beads of cold sweat sprang across her forehead. It appeared her mind also decided now was a good time to take a vacation. It refused to think about anything at all, forming no words or impressions, shut down.

She struggled not to give in to panic as her brain refused to form so much as a single opinion about the current state of affairs.

Jess tried passing the information through again.

I've been kidnapped.

Several long moments passed in tense silence as her whole body strained for a reaction, any reaction.

"It's quite obvious you've been kidnapped, dumbass," she finally snapped.

She snickered, this turning into a self-deprecating, nervous sort of laughter that died a swift and awkward death, as the stark reality of her situation took root.

She took a deep breath and ran her hands through her hair in an effort to still her shaking hands.

"It's ok. I'm ok." At this statement, she took a quick self-inventory to be sure.

There was a tiny puncture wound on the inside of her right arm, but since she didn't feel drugged decided not to think about it too much.

One thing at a time.

"Yeah, I'm fine. I'll be fine. I just have to escape, that's all," she reassured herself.

She climbed to her feet and took some more deep breaths. She could make coherent observations and theories, come up with a plan to escape and execute it. No, she *would*. She nodded to herself for emphasis.

Ok, so observations and theories.

Maybe the government had nabbed her to do weird, illegal experiments on her in some top-secret underground bunker? This wasn't some psycho's dump. Oh no, she wasn't chained to a rusty pipe in a garage or basement somewhere, with a weird smell permeating the air and the steady sound of water dripping in the background. She sniffed inquisitively.

Hm.

There was in fact no smell here aside from the faint scent of her own fear-fueled sweat.

She ground her teeth together.

No need to focus on that.

Alright, so no smell pointed to a well maintenanced industrial air filtration system. Though she didn't see any vents. The room appeared to be a perfectly sealed box with no openings of any kind.

Oh my god, am I going to suffocate to death?

Why would someone go to all the trouble to kidnap her, only to smother her in this room though?

No. There's got to be vents I just can't see them. Which is really weird but... What else?

Constructing steel rooms like this with top of the line ventilation had to be expensive as hell, right? If she was in some sort of compound as the room would indicate, safe to assume then that this was a well-funded, well organized operation. Which would definitely point to government. They were no doubt watching her every move, studying her, collecting data on her behavior or some bullshit.

Jess looked up and moved around the room, squinting to scrutinize the ceiling and corners. She looked for a camera or tiny blinking light or anything that would give her even the smallest clue.

But there was nothing she could see except for steel and more steel. There was no sign of a camera, but that didn't mean it wasn't there. It simply meant they didn't want it to be obvious. This still had the inhospitable, impersonal touch of the government all over it.

The glint of the light off the steel pierced her eyes to the point of pain if she looked at it for too long. Then again, there wasn't anything else to look at.

She rubbed her eyes, trying to get rid of the little black spots cavorting in front of them. She thought she had every chance of going more than a little mad in this soulless cell.

Maybe that's the point. They're trying *to make me go crazy in this absurd, dehumanizing room to study my reactions or…something. Well, screw that noise.*

She looked up at the middle of the ceiling. The only interruption to the cold, monotonous silver was a small square panel for the light. They could have hidden a camera in there. Also, she might be able to fit through it.

She rolled the gurney underneath the light and climbed on to it. She could now reach the light panel, so she pounded it with the side of her fist, hoping it would fly up into a crawl space she could access to escape. Like in the movies. People were always doing that shit, escaping through vents and ceiling panels and whatnot.

It didn't budge.

Of course not. You're not in *a movie Jess. Did you really think that would work?*

She continued to beat at it with her fist, hoping maybe it would crack like plastic.

Nothing happened whatsoever.

She was no expert, but it almost seemed harder than the steel, though it lacked the metallic quality of everything else.

Jess sighed and looked around the room from her vantage point atop the gurney, rubbing her fist. She could see the tiniest of gaps, if she squinted, running all along the room between the ceiling and walls.

There are the vents, apparently.

She climbed down off the gurney and took to pacing the few steps back and forth across the room.

She wasn't sure she wouldn't have preferred the psycho's basement, to this. At least then she might have been able to find a way out, chained or not. Given the choice of abduction scenarios, this one was about as low on her list as possible.

She laughed humorlessly.

No one gave me a choice though.

She hadn't even known she'd been kidnapped until she woke up. Whoever it was, they were good. Score another vote for the government theory.

But for god's sake, why?

She figured her life was about as average as you could get. She had no enemies that she could think of, so some kind of crazy revenge motive was out. There was nothing remarkable or different about her worth studying, that she was aware of. She was thoroughly, well, normal. How on Earth could she have gotten the attention of the government? There was just…no reason for this.

Well, this is a pointless line of thought. Moving on.

She stalled however, as she was unsure what kind of progress she'd made so far. She had concluded that this was some kind of government experiment.

Fine, that's great. Still have no idea what they want me for, but odds are it's not for anything good.

She shuddered.

She had observed that there didn't seem to be any way out of this room.

Fucking fantastic.

Well. Retrace events, that's supposed to help right? Ok, so last night.

It was clear she had been drugged. But how? When?

She absently rubbed the puncture mark on her arm.

She was pretty sure she would have noticed being stuck with a needle and woken up. So drugged first, then the shot of...whatever. That didn't necessarily make sense, but she moved on anyway.

Sure, she'd had a few drinks last night – it was Monday Girl's Night. But she had spaced out her drinks with glasses of water as usual, at a bar just a couple blocks from her apartment. She never had more than a few drinks because getting blitzed in public wasn't her style. Feeling out of control, even in familiar surroundings with familiar people was not something she enjoyed. She certainly hadn't been out of control last night and her memory of events wasn't the least bit fuzzy. Yeah she might drink often, but not in large quantities. She wasn't completely stupid.

She had played the customary rounds of darts with the girls and gone home. She'd walked back from the bar, taken a shower and even picked out her clothes for work tomorrow. Then she had snuggled under her covers safe and sound.

Nothing out of the ordinary had occurred at all. No one had confronted her and the few people she'd seen on the walk home hadn't gotten close enough to so much as brush up against her.

There was the typical Monday night crowd and no strangers or people that seemed out of place. Not that she'd been paying the utmost attention to minute details or anything, but it had still seemed like a regular Monday night. Surely she or one of her friends would have noticed something abnormal had it been going on, right?

No bumps in the night, no windows breaking, no drama. Not so much as a broken heel. Entirely normal.

Yet here she was.

God, I have to get out of here, she thought as panic hit her again.

She ran her hands along the walls, looking for any ridge, mark or crack that could indicate a door.

After thoroughly searching and re-searching and finding nothing but her own blurry reflection, she pushed away from the wall in irritation. While she knew there *had* to be a door here she sure as hell wasn't finding it.

Well great. Now what?

She paced back and forth again, becoming more agitated with each step.

Goddammit this is creepy.

No. Just focus, breathe.

She reluctantly sat on the stupid, pointless gurney.

Why would someone put this in here anyway? It's not like it's any softer than the floor. Ugh.

She kept mulling over the possibilities.

*Let's see…*so she couldn't pull off immediate escape. When would someone realize she was gone and investigate her disappearance?

She considered the potential state of her apartment. Maybe there was a broken window after all which would alert someone that something was wrong. So if there was a broken window, her super would investigate and… find no sign of struggle. There had been no struggle because she hadn't put up one.

The police wouldn't show up because no one would have called them in the first couple days, so the super would assume someone had done it while she was at work. He would simply fix the window and send her the bill.

Dammit.

Her boss wouldn't to call the police the minute she didn't show up for work. While she almost never missed work, her supervisor was more the type to assume she was slacking or sick rather than worry about her. She was pretty cold. As more time went by, she'd be more likely to fire her over the phone than to call her parents' number listed on the contact form.

So no hope there.

Her parents? She'd had her weekly phone conversation with them the evening before. So they wouldn't know she was gone for almost an entire week.

No steady boyfriend, her friends and co-workers would assume she was sick and not up for conversation when she didn't answer her cell.

She'd never had a problem with the casual, carefree nature of the relationships she had cultivated in her life. In fact, she'd enjoyed it.

Until now.

Her preference for space and the lack of personal responsibility that came with those kinds of relationships now felt like a weight on her chest, crushing her.

No one would tear the world apart looking for her. Her parents would certainly launch an investigation into her disappearance, but at some point they would have to return to their jobs and rely on the police to handle it. They would go back home, hundreds of miles away and the police would stop looking. She'd become another face sitting under big block letters pronouncing her "MISSING". People would avert their eyes, unwilling to think too long about the sad evidence of another young woman vanishing without a trace.

She swallowed the overwhelming wave of regret washing over her and ignored the self-pitying tears that stung her eyes.

Well, no use thinking any more about that now, when there was diddly squat she could do about it.

So no one would report her missing for a week or more. She was alone and likely to stay that way. No one was coming to save her from this nightmare.

I am screwed.

"No, I can't think that!" she shouted, jumping off the gurney. "I *refuse* to think that!"

She winced as the sound reverberated around the room at a startling volume, then seethed for a few moments, and gave herself a defiant stare-down.

Somehow, she would just have to get herself out of this situation.

Think.

She took a couple deep breaths.

Right. Eventually, someone had to come to do…whatever with her. She would attack them the minute they stepped through wherever the hell the door was and she'd be gone. She'd be fine.

A couple of friends had convinced her to take a self-defense class a few years back, so she knew where to hit and how to leverage her weight and all that. She could do this.

As a matter of fact, she would take pleasure in attacking these assholes! So who cared that no one was coming to her rescue?

So there's that. A plan.

The only other thing left to contemplate was the reason she had been abducted and brought here. Her mind reared away from that question.

I can't think about that. I will go crazy.

She laughed then, as hysteria threatened to bubble to the surface.

Maybe I am crazy. Ooh, maybe I did something I can't remember and I'm in some kind of hospital to prevent me from hurting myself or others.

Then she thought it was a little pathetic that was something she was actually kind of hoping for at this point. Still, it would be preferable to a lot of other scenarios.

Eh. Let's just put that on the back burner.

How long would she be kept here, without even knowing why? How long had she been in here? She would guess it had been around an hour since she woke up.

Suddenly, she snapped. Rationality and logic melted away as her fear and fury boiled over with impromptu viciousness.

She screamed as she pounded on the walls until she couldn't make a fist anymore, then tried kicking them. That didn't last too long, with her bare feet. She howled with impotent fury, ignoring the fact that her own screaming echoed right back at her, hurting her ears.

Then she thought the gurney could be useful after all and she could somehow reveal a seam in the metal if she hit the right spot with it, so she decided to ram it into the walls.

She started really getting into it, experimenting with different angles and speeds, different areas.

After about half an hour of this and not so much as a single dent or scratch in either the walls or the gurney itself, she stopped.

Nothing, she thought as she stood there, panting. *That did nothing.*

No one came rushing in to stop her, no alarm went off. There wasn't one mark to show her thirty minutes of unbridled fury had ever occurred. Not one. This couldn't even be steel, which would have at the very least been scratched. Something much stronger then - what - she had no clue.

She sank into a corner, deflated. She sat there, staring at her reflection on the opposite wall.

"Now what?" she asked her image. "Now fucking what?"

The only thing she could determine as being potentially effective, as she'd thought before, would be to attack whoever came for her and flee for her life. So she would fight like her life depended on it. For all she knew, it very well might.

So she settled in to wait.

Eventually someone will come. Someone will come…the thought repeated in her head like a mantra. It kept the other, less welcome thoughts at bay.

After what she estimated to be about two hours passed, in a combination of mind numbing tedium and tense vigilance, she heard a slight hiss from the wall on her right.

Jess leaped to her feet and prepared to rush whoever came into the room.

A normal door shaped section emerged the slightest bit from the wall into the room and slid aside.

What the hell, she thought, before shooing away the utter weirdness of that as nothing but a distraction.

She crouched down, balanced on the balls of her feet and prepared to spring.

Someone stepped through the door.

Right as she was about to launch herself, her eyes widened in shock as she got a good look at what had walked into her room. Instead of launching she gasped and instantly backtracked away from the entrance.

"No, this isn't…you can't…" she said in a voice thickened by the overwhelming need to shriek with disbelief.

She held her hands out in front of her in an unconscious effort to stave off the reality of what she saw, and continued to back away from the door.

Another one entered behind the first.

"Please remain calm. You will not be harmed, unless you pose a threat," the first one said.

She bumped into the wall behind her, shaking her head in denial.

Not able to hold it in any longer, she let out an ear piercing scream.

CHAPTER TWO

They glanced at each other with what she somehow registered as impatience, as she stood wedged as far as she could get into the corner.

How dare they be impatient with me, they completely ruined my only chance to escape by being fucking aliens!

At least that's sure as hell what they looked like to her.

Oh my god, they're aliens. Wait, aliens?

The last word replayed over and over, whirling drunkenly around in her brain trying to find anything to anchor itself to. Her mind latched onto the improbability and ran with it.

No. That's absurd. It's probably just some dickbags in a costume, or they've drugged me and I'm hallucinating. Assholes!

Without further thought, she charged.

Before she took two steps, the first one whipped out some sort of gun - out of god knew where - and shot her.

The gun produced a shock wave which instantly paralyzed her. Her knees buckled and she pitched forward.

One of the 'aliens' leapt forward to catch her as she collapsed.

She would have recoiled in alarm if she could have, instead her head lolled back over his - or its - arm.

The other one grabbed her legs, and they placed her on the gurney with surprising care.

This can't be happening, this absolutely can't *be happening. I have been kidnapped by assholes posing as fucking aliens. This is beyond sick…*

Ok, but, then where they hell did they get that damn gun?

Either way, she would need a description for police, so she reviewed every detail of their costumes. Or makeup, whatever it was. They seemed to have gone to a lot of trouble, she had never seen anything like it in her life.

Their skin had the appearance of bark, though it was a silvery-beige color. Mottled and patterned with traces of dark pewter running across long, lean muscles. She imagined the patterns were both unique, but not only hadn't really noticed, also didn't give a flying shit.

Must have taken hours and hours of professional work though. They are serious about their little farce.

They were both very tall, which was peculiar. Around seven feet if she had to guess, which she did, currently being without a tape measure and *fucking paralyzed.*

Their foreheads swept back and up from their eyes in a strange manner, with a tall, squarish cranial structure that dominated their faces. They had something between a typical 'human' nose and a smooth bulge with two holes in it. It gave them a vaguely piggish look.

How appropriate.

They appeared hairless with smooth skin. She wanted to say they were male based on the voice of the one that spoke. But they might have had some kind of voice changing device, too.

She would have laughed then if she could move.

Like their gender matters. I'm incapacitated on this fucking gurney, in a steel box - in space - according to their little charade.

Oh my god, maybe I'm in space! Wait, that would not be good at all. Shit, what is going on here?

Her eyes involuntarily teared up.

Alright Jess, keep it together.

The worst part was their eyes - completely white with no pupil or iris.

They had taken care of every detail and the result was the creepiest thing she had ever seen.

She tried to wrack her brain for more details. Hands, feet, what were they like? God, she couldn't remember looking directly at their hands and definitely hadn't looked at their feet. She had been rather preoccupied, what with the terrified screaming going on and all.

Unhinged laughter floated through her skull.

One of them finally spoke, interrupting her little internal monologue.

"Approximately two hundred years ago, our race realized we were failing to reproduce at a sufficient rate to ensure the survival of our species. It became apparent that if we could not start expanding our numbers, we would die out within a matter of a few hundred years. Our infrastructures would fall apart and our societies would crumble. The few left would take to killing each other and we would cease to exist."

Good, go die you kidnapping bastards, I hope you cease to exist. Like, right now.

She tried to ignore the unease that skittered down her immobile spine.

"We introduced a worldwide fertility program on our home planet. Our technology was promising, and we had every hope it would provide a solution."

The building disquiet she'd felt when they had mentioned reproduction eased a bit.

But for shit's sake, then what did they want her for? Were they going to just study her and 'probe' her or whatever and take her back home?

She snickered to herself. She could maybe live with that. Maybe they would just extract her ovaries or…?

God, what do they want, why can't they just get to the freaking point?

"At first we had some mixed results but continued to make adjustments to the program, seeking the right combination of methods and procedures."

Aren't you special? Do you want a goddamn medal?

Jess screamed at her body to move, to no avail. She tried to wiggle her fingers and toes. Nothing happened. She had no control.

How long will I be disabled like this?

"We found we could increase the chances of successfully inseminating our females, though it required enormous resources of time and a certain rare mineral on our home planet. The material enhanced the hormonal receptivity response of a statistically promising number of our females for specific limited time periods, allowing carefully selected unions to be fruitful. However this was an intricate, delicate process that provided results unsatisfactory to the general arc of the program's goals - to provide a sustainable solution to our reproduction failures. And not all the females responded to the program."

Ahh, so you are probably males. So typical, blaming everything on the women.

She noticed he…it, whatever, spoke slowly and methodically, pausing every so often. Like it was trying to remember lines, or was unused to its own voice.

She couldn't see either of them as they both stood off to her right side, in between her and the door. She couldn't even move her eyes.

"After several rounds of experimentation over the course of a few decades, the fertility program was ultimately unsuccessful. When the required materials began to run out and our species came no closer to an acceptable solution, we decided another approach might yield more satisfactory results."

The unease was back.

"We launched a space program to seek other species that might be capable of cross-mating with our own."

Oh my god. You two are so cracked.

"We did not achieve adequate results for many years. We found a few species who were willing to negotiate, but they turned out to be incompatible. Another species was unwilling to negotiate but was a potential match for the program. So we proceeded with the program, without a specific treaty or terms. However, they turned out to have hybridization barriers that became problematic. So we continued the search."

Congratufuckinglations to you!

"Eventually, we found Earth."

She lay there like a carcass, unwillingly staring at the ceiling.

"After our sample program proved humans capable of hybridization, we observed. We looked for indications that the inhabitants of the planet would be willing to negotiate and fulfill a cross-breeding treaty. Unfortunately, we observed that humans are a destructive race which creates war where it shouldn't exist and barely tolerates the variations in your own species. To be more precise, you *don't* tolerate your own variations. You routinely kill each other over your differences though they are irrelevant. We concluded that you would be unwilling to procreate with what you perceived to be 'aliens'. You have weapons capable of mass destruction. Our council convened and decided the risk of failed negotiations was too great and could result in unpredictable consequences."

I will show you unpredictable consequences, she vowed.

"In light of all this, the fact remains that yours is the only race we have found capable of hybridization without exception. Our genetic composition is remarkably similar, not unlike the superficial differences between your species and *Homo neanderthalensis.* Therefore, willing or…otherwise we approved the interbreeding program with humans. We regret that there is no other way, but understand that our survival depends on it. You possess qualities acceptable to us in terms of genetic inheritance. Brown hair, blue eyes, proportionate features that humans would describe as attractive. You are of slim build and are tall…enough, for a human female at five feet eight inches. This is especially desirable, since our race is much taller than yours and that has in the past proven, problematic, shall we say. Your initial scan reveals no undesirable hereditary diseases or conditions that you may pass to a child, and you are in peak health. Therefore, you have been selected as a participant. You received the appropriate hormones upon arrival and the subsequent scan revealed your body is prepared for reproduction. You will be inseminated, carry the child to term, give birth and then be returned to your planet to resume your normal activities."

At that, they both turned and silently left the room. The door hissed shut.

She laid there, stunned.

The words *you will be inseminated* roared in her ears repeatedly.

A single tear escaped from her frozen eye socket and rolled down her temple.

CHAPTER THREE

Jess laid there alternately fuming and despairing for about another half hour, until the effects of the paralysis wore off.

She wiggled her toes and flexed her fingers, then shifted her arms and legs until she felt like she'd be able to control her muscles again. It took a couple of tries, but within a few minutes the last vestiges of immobility faded and she propped herself up.

She sat there for a moment, trying to absorb everything the 'aliens' had told her, then, with a snort of disgust she edged off the gurney and took a few cautious steps.

This is absolutely, out of this world, bat-shit crazy.
*Out of this world…*she snickered.

But the reality surrounded her and the facts were smacking her right in the face. Literally. With a stun gun.

It was therefore irrelevant what she wanted to believe. And her reality currently indicated she had indeed been...*fucking abducted by aliens*.

Jess curled herself into the corner. She refused to sit on the gurney anymore. She also discovered it was hard to concentrate with the slight echo of her breathing grating on her nerves.

God, what the hell am I supposed to do *in here? They couldn't have given me something to read or look at or something*?

Her brain again appeared reluctant to function. The events of the last couple of hours seemed to all rush in at her at once, overwhelming her capacity to think at a normal level. Her thoughts were a maelstrom that refused to settle on one thing in the cacophony of random feelings and concepts. Despite the half hour 'time out' she still had no idea what to make of this whole situation. She had nothing to compare it to.

She decided that maybe the best thing for her right now was to take a little nap. Perhaps it would be better to let her mind take some time to absorb all...this. Preferably while she was unconscious. She slid down onto her side, closed her eyes and attempted to sleep.

She must have dozed because what seemed like minutes later, the hiss of the door startled her and she shot up, scrambling backwards into the corner.

She didn't want to be shot with that damned gun again. Plus, she thought she might lull them into complacency if she didn't try anything for a while.

The 'alien' stood in the doorway with a tray in its hands.

It knelt down, placed the tray on the floor and slid it a couple feet into the room.

"Hey!" she shouted, then winced as the echo hit her ears.

She leapt to her feet.

"What are you doing? What is this? How long am I gonna be in here?!"

It stared at her for the briefest of seconds with its blank, creepy eyes then stepped back out of the doorway.

"*Hey!*" she tried again.

The door closed.

"Goddamn aliens!" she screamed, before being reminded yet again why it was such a bad idea to yell in this room.

She rubbed her ears, trying to rid them of the ringing.

Jess walked over to the tray and stared down at it skeptically. It looked like an egg and cheese sandwich, a container of strawberries and grapes, a plate of sliced cucumbers and a bottle of water.

She did a double take, which might have been funny to her had the situation been any different than it was.

Evian? Are you kidding me?

The sheer normalcy of seeing a recognizable brand name right in front of her, taunting her, was almost more than she could process alongside everything else.

She shook her head in amazement and her stomach growled as if on cue.

Well if everything they told me was true, she thought with a shudder, *it's unlikely this is poisoned.*

She sat down in front of the tray, picked up the sandwich and sniffed suspiciously. It smelled delicious.

She shrugged. She would need her strength if she was going to try to get away from these lanky bastards so she could get the hell out of here.

She tucked into the food with vigor and finished off the entire plate in a few minutes. Then she grabbed the water and stood up to stretch.

After she downed half the water, a couple crucial bits of information she hadn't considered before suddenly hit her like a gut punch.

How am *I going to get out of here? If I'm in goddamn space –not that I really believe that - how am I going to get off the ship? Find my way home?*

Ok, say they really *were* aliens. They had to have like, travel pods or whatever, they'd just brought her normal Earth food. But even if they did, she knew exactly nothing about flying a spaceship, navigating her way back to Earth, or anything else that escaping might require.

Then, as if it had been waiting for the perfect moment, the thought of how they would accomplish her insemination reared up to the forefront of her mind.

Without warning, the entire contents of her stomach emptied onto the floor. She stood bent over for a few moments with her hands on her knees and retched until there was nothing left to bring back up.

Oh my god, I am so fucked.

She took a deep, shaky breath and spat the lingering taste of bile out of her mouth.

No goddammit, you can't think like that. And definitely *don't think about what they plan to do to you. That won't do anything besides turn you into a neurotic mess and you'll be useless.*

She firmly set aside all the disturbing images her mind had conjured up and refocused.

Maybe they were lying to her about 'returning her to her planet' and they were in fact still on Earth. They wanted her to think that escape was impossible so she wouldn't attempt it. Because she *could*.

They're assholes so that is totally something they would do. Probably. So maybe just bide your time, let them believe you are harmless, helpless and docile. Alright, we'll call that Plan A.

She settled into the corner again to focus on constructing the best plan options she could. No point in having only one.

After about another half hour passed with her plotting her escape, the now familiar hiss of the door interrupted her train of thought.

One of them stepped into the room holding some kind of cloth. It looked over at her expressionlessly as far as she could tell and she gave it a placid smile, trying her best to look meek.

It paused - she assumed to study her for signs of aggression - and then walked over to the puke covered tray and bent down to clean up the mess.

Yeah clean up after me asshole.

That it had come prepared also told her they *were* watching her.

It finished cleaning and stepped out of the room to put the tray somewhere outside the door, keeping her in sight. Then it walked back into the room carrying a five gallon bucket with a little toilet seat on it and a roll of toilet paper.

She couldn't help the glare she suspected had taken over her face.

It placed the items in the corner opposite her and with one last glance at her, left the room.

Oh great, not only are they observing me, they'll be watching me do my business on a freaking bucket toilet. Lovely. I'll just put that on my long, ever growing "Things That Suck About Being Abducted By Aliens" list.

Her stomach rumbled again, in protest of being given food just to have it immediately taken away.

Tough shit stomach, guess you shouldn't have rejected the food over a case of nerves. Right...case of nerves, that's one way to put it.

She sighed.

Work on Plan B I suppose.

She flipped the gurney over to inspect it. There didn't appear to be any exposed screws or bolts anywhere that she could use to fashion into a weapon.

God, how is this thing even staying together?

Everything was smooth joints. The legs seemed to vanish into the top without so much as a hint of welding and the wheels were countersunk into the legs somehow.

Now I hate this thing even more.

She sighed again. So much for that brilliant idea.

She sat down dispiritedly to wait for the next appearance, which she assumed would be lunch time.

Time dragged by and she began to question her Plan A: waiting for them let their guard down. She wasn't sure she had the patience. Not here, not now.

Screw this appearing docile bullshit, she decided after another couple hours passed. *Plan C: the next time one of those sons of bitches comes in here, I'm going for it.*

Hours passed with excruciating slowness. She felt like she would go insane from sheer boredom.

Her stomach began to rumble with increased vigor so she got to her feet and paced as she waited for the whisper of the door to announce her next unlucky visitor.

She didn't wait long. The sound she had been anticipating echoed through the room. She tensed and edged towards the door.

One of their stun guns appeared from the other side of the entrance, pointed straight at her.

Shit. So much for Plan C.

"Move away from the door or I will shoot you," said a voice from around the corner.

She backed away with a small, disappointed frown and he...it - whatever - stepped into the room. She didn't feel like being paralyzed again and apparently her jig was up.

With the gun still pointed at her, another one walked in and tried to grab her arm.

She narrowly dodged it and took a step backwards.

"What are you doing?" she asked, incredulous.

She gave it her deadliest glare.

It went for her arm again, and she backed away again.

It went for her arm a third time and succeeded.

She yanked her arm out its grasp.

"*I said,* what are you doing?!" She was amazed they hadn't shot her yet. "You guys are rude as hell, you know that? Why do you keep trying to gr-"

Her tirade was cut off as it snatched her arm and dragged her out of the room before she even had time to gather another breath.

Damn, they're quick.

She was about to carry on with her tirade but was distracted by the immense hallway she had been hauled into.

Good god.

If the hallways were any indication of the size of this place, it was massive. She gulped.

Then, refusing to be intimidated, decided to keep trying to pump them for information. Sure, it had been a fruitless endeavor up to this point, but maybe she would at the least annoy one of them enough to slip up and respond to her.

"Are you two male or female?" She waited.

Nothing.

"Where are you taking me?"

Silence.

Oddly enough, despite the echo in her room, in this hallway it was as if the walls absorbed sound. She didn't even hear footsteps.

Reminded, she looked down at their feet, but couldn't see anything past their long white gowns.

Of course not.

"Where are we? We're not even in space are we? C'mon give it up man, you're not aliens. Admit it, you're just two assholes with great costumes and a professional makeup artist on board with your ridiculous little game."

Still nothing.

They continued to traverse the hallway.

Man, they seem to have an absolute love affair with the steel look.

Steel stretched down the hall as far as the eye could see.

After a short walk, they turned a corner to reveal another steel corridor.

Shocker.

"What's up with you guys and steel anyways?"

Predictably, nothing.

"Say nothing if you are the scum of the universe!"

Haa. Well, they hadn't disagreed.

"For real guys, where are you taking me? If you don't answer me this time, I will scream."

"Please remain calm, everything will be alright."

"Are you fucking kidding me? That's your only response? *Please remain calm, everything will be alright?*" she sneered back at the one on left who'd spoken.

"Please remain calm."

"Fuck no I'm not gonna remain calm! Not until you assholes tell me where you're taking me!"

"Everything will be alright."

"Hoooly shit, I'm dealing with the biggest morons in existence here."

Nothing. Great, we're back to this again.

"How far are we from Earth? Where did you come from? Do you have names? How the hell am I supposed to tell you apart, you all look the same, ugly!"

She cackled at her own joke. They kept walking silently.

"So did it take you guys years of practice to become the biggest dicks in the galaxy, or did it just happen naturally?"

She laughed again.

Hey, at least I'm amusing myself.

Abruptly, they stopped and turned to the right.

The one that wasn't holding her took a step towards what looked to be a blank, unremarkable portion of the wall. It looked like every single *other* inch of wall in the hallways. That is to say, steel. Endless, uninterrupted steel.

After doing nothing as far as she could tell aside from standing there in front of the wall for a few moments, she heard the telltale hiss of a door opening.

The other one tugged her toward the doorway and shoved her through it. She stumbled into the incredibly bright room half blinded, and the panel closed behind her.

CHAPTER FOUR

She peered out from behind the arm she'd automatically raised to shield her eyes from the intense glare. All she could handle looking at for the moment was the floor, to try to allow her eyes to adjust to the ridiculous lighting situation.

Holy god what were they trying to do, replicate the effing sun?

She slowly lowered her arm and saw five of them in the room, standing around...another fucking gurney?

Oh this isn't going to go well.

Behind them was another steel (*what else?*) table with different tools and containers and such on it.

She swallowed hard.

This was beginning to look all too real. It seemed increasingly implausible that there would be this many people, all of the same general height - really damn tall - in full prosthetics and makeup, going along with…whatever this was.

"What is all this then?" she said with a wave of her hand in their direction, still squinting against the light.

"Please remain cal-"

"Yeah yeah, I know, please remain calm, blah fucking blah. I asked you a question asshole, how bout you answer it for a change? I *said*, what is all this about then?"

"You will be inseminated now."

"Nope," she said succinctly as she turned around and pounded on the 'door' behind her, which she could no longer see but assumed was the right spot.

A hand descended on her shoulder.

"Don't touch me!" she screeched and jerked away. "Don't fucking touch me!"

One of them nearby murmured what sounded like "We have another combative one."

"Hell yes you have another combative one!" She continued to pound on the smooth wall.

She felt a hand once more on her shoulder and jerked away again.

"Get your hands off me asshole! If you think this is gonna go down like this and I'm not gonna have a problem with it, you've got another thing coming!"

"Please remain calm Jess-"

"Don't you dare! Don't you *dare* use my name, you don't get to do that!"

"If you can please remain calm, the procedure will take but a few minutes and oomph-"

She'd swiftly turned around and jump kicked it for all she was worth in what she assumed was its stomach…area. If they even had stomachs.

It quickly recovered and stretched back out to its full height.

Shit, why do they have to be so damn tall?

"Grab her," said the one she had kicked.

"Uh-uh. No one's gonna be grabbing any-"

Two of them flanked her, each taking one of her arms and simply lifting her off her feet.

She shrieked and tried swinging around to kick them in the soft areas. She thought she made some good contact once or twice, but it didn't seem to have any impact at all.

Fuck!

They carried her over to the gurney and after a few moments of difficulty, slammed her down onto it. Her teeth clacked together painfully as she landed and the breath was knocked out of her.

She lay briefly stunned, then resumed her struggle.

The two who held her arms tried to keep her down as she attempted to squirm her way off the gurney and kicked out violently to make it as difficult as possible for the other two to grab her legs.

However, they did eventually get a hold of both legs, leaning on them with their weight to keep them immobile. She was utterly amazed that they hadn't shot her with that gun yet.

She continued to scream.

This isn't real, this isn't real, this can't *be real*.

She bucked and twisted and tried not to think about how their skin didn't feel human at all. It had a cool, scaly feel and an odd oily powder-like substance rubbed off onto her skin.

"Tie her down so we may proceed," said the only one so far that hadn't been engaged in the brawl. He seemed to be calling the shots.

She screamed louder, swearing and cursing them with every breath.

Occasionally, one of them would mutter "please remain calm", and she responded with a scream as close to their face as she could get. They didn't seem to like loud noise very much.

She nearly succeeded in head butting one of them at one point, but it reared back at the last second.

Straps appeared and they began the arduous task of trying to tie her down. She also made this as difficult as possible. She kicked, screamed and flailed with all her might.

Finally though, her arms and legs were tied down, so she continued to scream and struggle against the straps. Maybe she could loosen them and knock one of these fuckers out somehow.

"Please silence her, it will be a distraction to the procedure."

A wad of cloth was shoved into her mouth, though this was accomplished with some difficulty as every time one of got close enough to her face, she tried biting them. She almost managed it once.

A strip around her head followed and the cloth was tied in place. She kept screaming anyway, hoping at the very least all this would put them in a bad mood for the rest of the day. She knew she would be.

Four of them now put their weight on her to reduce her movement even further. She began to wear out then, but persisted in screaming behind the gag.

Within about thirty seconds, she felt probing between her legs.

Though they had told her this was the general direction events were headed, her eyes widened in shock and she renewed her efforts. The aliens just leaned on her more, one of them pressing its body across her chest.

She turned her face away from it and squeezed her eyes shut, as if she could shut out the reality of what was happening to her.

Her pants and then her underwear were cut up the middle and laid aside, the chilly air of the room immediately flowing over the exposed area. Her face went furiously red with embarrassment. She screamed now with everything she had, to little effect behind the muffling cloth.

After a brief pause, something entered her and she felt pressure as her canal was spread open. A tube was inserted, past her cervix-which pinched a bit, followed by a small fluidic rush deep inside her.

Her eyes flew open and she abruptly stopped screaming. Too shocked to do much of anything now, she stared in disbelief at the wall.

It happened so fast that, as mentally prepared as she thought she was, she was wrong. She hadn't been prepared at all.

The tube was removed and something else was placed inside her. She barely registered it, though it seemed to take longer than anything else had up to this point. Everything now seemed to happen from an odd distance and her mind drifted away from the movements around her.

Her leg restraints were loosened and some kind of wedge shaped thing was placed under her, then the straps were pulled tight again.

They placed the implements on the table and silently retreated from the room, the hiss of the door opening and closing the only sound to mark their departure. She stared at the ceiling as they exited, leaving her exposed and still open, her lower half now tilted slightly upward on the table.

After about half an hour of her laying stunned and motionless on the gurney, they returned.

One of them bent down, bringing its eye level to her exposed region and reached in to remove the last object they had put in her. Her face automatically flushed again at the scrutiny and subsequent intrusion, then she felt the pressure ease as the spreader was removed. Though she flinched slightly, she didn't otherwise move or do anything.

They removed the wedge and untied her. She continued to lay there, somewhat sore from the prolonged stretching. She was too defeated to muster the will to move.

Two of them hefted her into a sitting position, then eased her off the gurney. They supported her as she stood there for a moment, swaying.

Then they ushered her out of the room and she walked mechanically through the corridors back to her room. She felt some cramping and a wetness rubbing between her thighs, now bare thanks to her shredded pajamas.

She made a moue of disgust but immediately shoved any other thought about it out of her head and refused to think about the fact she was walking down the hall with essentially her whole private area exposed. Her skin was covered in the oily powder substance from their skin and there was nothing she could do to get it off.

They pushed her into the cell and the door closed behind them.

She just stood there for a few long minutes, the silence ringing in her ears. Eventually she made her way over to the corner and slid down into it.

She stared unseeing at the wall in front of her.

CHAPTER FIVE

Days passed in a haze of monotony.

The arrival of her food and the replacement of her toilet bucket were the only events that marked the passage of time.

Jess generally picked over her food listlessly, sometimes eating and sometimes doing nothing more than crumbling, shredding or squishing it into unrecognizable piles. She lost weight, her slender physique taking on a gaunt, almost skeletal appearance.

She'd tried as best she could to knot the cut ends of her pants together so she wasn't constantly flashing the...aliens bringing her food.

It took a full week before she could get through their appearances without her face heating uncomfortably. Soon, she stopped feeling much of anything. She had come to the realization that she was in some very deep shit. Her abductors gave every indication that they were, in fact, not human.

She began to talk to herself out loud, in soft tones, in an effort to keep her mind from shattering completely. Though she wasn't sure she was accomplishing that, it seemed preferable to listening to nothing but her echoed breathing for hours without end.

She held long conversations with herself, her friends, her family. She told them about what had happened to her and tried to imagine their responses.

What she couldn't picture was anyone actually believing her. She would get sympathetic, worried glances and gentle yet pointed questions about what had 'really' happened.

They would tell her she could 'tell them the truth' when she was ready. She was just traumatized from the whole ordeal and her subconscious had constructed an elaborate fantasy scenario as a way to cope. It was understandable as something clearly *had* happened to her, they could get her some help and so on. But she was pretty sure that she was well beyond 'help'.

She tried to think of ways she could prove any of this. If these aliens would indeed let her go back home after she had…the baby, an exam would prove that. But it would prove that she had given birth, and nothing more. It certainly wouldn't prove that she had given birth to an *alien* baby.

She thought she read something a while ago about DNA being left behind in the mother's body after giving birth. So maybe she could have whatever test that involved and it would prove her story when they found alien DNA in her body. Right? So that was a possibility.

But how had everyone missed the fact that these goddamn aliens are here in the first place?

She couldn't be the first woman they had done this to. Or to have thought about this DNA thing. How many women had become victims to these fuckers? Dozens? Hundreds? Thousands?

After that little speech, she highly doubted it was just her. Someone had to have said something before now, she just hadn't heard about it.

That thought kind of made its own point. There were a lot of crazy people out there who claimed all sorts of ridiculous things. Although now, some of those things seemed a whole lot less ridiculous.

I just can't fathom how these assholes are getting away with this.

How had all the world's governments somehow missed their presence in the space around Earth, with SETI and loads of other organizations observing said space? Or missed them when they came to Earth to do their abducting? They weren't exactly inconspicuous.

Jess went back and forth with herself in this manner endlessly. But she never really reached any solid conclusions.

She devised a way to mark the days by tying threads from her shirt around a leg of the gurney. She marked the days by counting the meals, because the light was always on. Her sense of day and night vanished completely.

According to her little calendar it was two weeks before an alien came into her room again, grabbed her arm and hauled her to her feet.

Taken by surprise with the change in the dull routine she'd become not exactly accustomed to, so much as numbed by, she complacently went along with it. She couldn't find the energy to bother asking it any questions this time.

It led her through the steel corridors, turning here and there until it stopped before a portion of the wall. The wall moved aside as usual, to reveal what appeared to be a bathroom.

Thank god.

Her own smell had begun to nauseate her, even though she hadn't been doing anything aside from sit around on a steel floor talking to herself. She had long ago learned to force out thoughts of the substances all over and in her body from the violation she had suffered.

She left her tattered clothes where they fell and stepped under what she guessed was the shower portion of the room. It had a pebbled texture on the floor and a bunch of small holes in the ceiling, which spouted lukewarm water onto her head. Of course they wouldn't even allow her to have hot water.

She sighed deeply at the feel of the water flowing over her skin and stood motionless for a good five minutes, reveling in the sensation.

Finally though, she decided it was probably a good idea to look for whatever passed as soap here. She noticed a little ledge holding what looked like a regular bar of soap, so she picked it up. She turned it over in her hand saw the word *Dial* etched into it.

She snorted with disbelief.

Of course its Dial. These aliens apparently love to mind fuck the women they abduct with these little snapshots of home.

God, I hate them. I really, really hate them.

She placed the soap back on its ledge and wrapped her arms around herself to stem the unwelcome flow of feelings that coursed through her.

Before she knew it tears were rolling down her face, barely distinguishable from the water that rained down gently onto her head. Broken sobs erupted from her then and she cried uncontrollably for several minutes, until she felt prickles on the back of her neck warning her she wasn't alone anymore.

She turned to find an alien standing about fifteen feet away from her, silently watching.

Well that's not creepy as hell.

She hastily wiped her dripping face and turned her back to it, covering her chest.

"Leave," she croaked. "Just leave me alone."

She looked over her shoulder to find it continued to stand there, staring at her.

"Go away!" she screamed at it. "Go away, go away, go away!"

"Please remain calm. It is time to return to your room."

"I'm not finished," she said in a small voice.

"You are finished, it is time to return to your room."

"But I didn't even wash yet."

She half turned towards it to give it a pleading look.

"You have used the resources allotted to you. You are finished."

It continued to gaze at her with its blank, white eyes. Without pupils, she couldn't tell precisely where it was looking.

"Can you at least turn around so I can get dressed in privacy?"

It just stood there motionless, eyes fixed on her.

Asshole.

"Fine, what am I supposed to wear?" she snapped.

It motioned to a small steel bench on her left.

With a glance over at the bench she saw a folded white garment laying on top of it.

She walked over and grabbed it one handed, trying to cover herself with the other arm. She turned her back to the alien and pulled the shapeless white dress over her head.

The alien grabbed for her arm but she dodged it.

"I can walk on my own you know, you don't need to hold my arm."

She raised her chin, daring it with her eyes to have a problem with her asserted self-authority.

It turned without another word so she followed it out of the bathroom and back to her cell.

After that bit of 'excitement', she settled back into her routine. Which was doing absolutely nothing.

Another week passed with the usual rounds of food, water and toilet replacement. She began to go more than a little stir crazy.

Several times she'd worked up the will to ask the alien that brought her food for something to do. This request was unvaryingly met with a blank stare and total silence.

Then an alien came into her room again and leaned down to grab her arm.

Habits are hard to break, I guess.

"Now what?" she spit as it tugged her up to her feet.

Nothing.

Oh, what a surprise, another uncommunicative one.

It dragged her through the hallways.

This shit has got to stop. What are they fucking cavemen for real?

It stopped in front of a random portion of wall and a door opened, then pushed her through the entry and the door closed behind her

This time as she looked around, the contents of the room were immediately recognizable. And her jaw dropped in absolute amazement.

CHAPTER SIX

The room was filled with women.

Some stood in clusters here and there, but many took advantage of the size of the room to get in some walking. Numerous groups circled the room in processions of twos and threes.

Large overstuffed couches in a rainbow of colors lined the walls of the cavernous room, with tables in between. The presence of color and variety alone was overwhelming.

Predictably she saw no windows, but potted trees and plants were spaced around the room in an attempt to give the room a welcoming atmosphere.

She stood there in awe, mouth still agape as her brain tried to process the sight of so many people in one place. In this place.

This is like…the ultimate harem. For aliens.
Ew.

After the previous weeks with nothing to keep her company but the sound of her own breathing and occasional ramblings, she felt a little dizzy from the mental effort of absorbing everything. The assault on her senses *almost* made her wish she was back in her cell, occupying the corner.

No, that's ridiculous.

She shook her head and continued to look around.

There has to be three hundred women in this room!

She spotted women from what seemed like every continent on Earth.

God, how is this possible?

While she'd concluded she probably wasn't alone in her abduction, this was incredible. The scale, unbelievable.

More women than she would have guessed were using the couches and corners to discreetly make love to each other. She shrugged and mentally wished them well.

Maybe it's helping them to cope with all this shit at least. Tenacity of the human spirit and all that.

She stood there for a few more minutes until she noticed a group of about ten women off to her right, one of them waving to her.

Waving? What is this Junior High?

She shook her head again, told herself to snap out of it and decided she might as well go over.

What else am I gonna do?

Upon reaching the group, she realized she didn't know what to say.

Am I really going to stand here and just…chit chat with these women? How am I supposed to do *that, after everything?*

She was surrounded by women in multiple stages of pregnancy, some more obvious than others. She tried to avoid the realization that she was most likely pregnant as well, but was rather unsuccessful at that particular moment. Every single one of them was a reminder of what they had done to her, to them, and what else she could 'look forward' to.

Eight more months of this fucking circus.

She already felt like she was becoming a little cracked. Jess ground her teeth together.

Uh-uh, nope, don't think like that. Let's try to remain positive shall we? Focus on what can be done instead of what's already happened and can't be changed. So, perhaps something can come of this new development. Maybe I'll be able to somehow rally these women together, get details, plan an escape. Pull a Spartacus or…something.

As Jess stood there anxiously, she tried to think of a way to start a group discussion along these lines.

The lack of conversation quickly became awkward and several of the women exchanged dubious glances with each other.

She had the belated thought that her silent concentration on internal musings might have translated as intense glaring. Or at the very least - resting bitch face. So she tried to rearrange her face into a more amiable expression. It had been awhile since she had even briefly considered what she might look like to someone else.

She lifted her hand to her hair to make it more presentable before remembering that she hadn't washed it in almost a month. To worry about what it looked like at this point was an exercise in futility. Greasy and frizzy didn't begin to describe it. She knew because of the hours she'd spent staring at her distorted metallic reflection, arranging and rearranging her hair to try to occupy herself.

She slowly lowered her hand.

Finally, the blonde who had waved her over tried to cover the tension.

She smiled up at Jess, being much shorter, and her blue eyes crinkled at the corners.

"I'm Amy. What's your name hon?" She spoke with a southern accent.

"Um, hi Amy. I'm Jess."

She realized her fists were clenched, so she self-consciously unclenched them. She didn't know why she was this tense.

Amazing what three weeks of total isolation will do to your people skills I guess.

And she worked in retail, she should have people skills coming out of her ass. She snorted.

"I'm sorry hon, did you say something?" Amy inquired politely.

"No, I'm sorry. I…don't know what to say here. It's not like this is a freaking ice cream social or something..." she trailed off awkwardly.

C'mon Jess, focus. Ask your questions. Rally dammit! Fucking Spartacus!

"Well, it's nice to meet you, Jess."

"Really? I wish I could say the same. I mean, no offense or anything but I'd rather never have met you."

Ok, what had happened to her filter? She was usually an expert filterer.

They all bobbed their heads uncomfortably and Amy averted her eyes, the barest hint of a blush coloring her fair skin.

Ugh, now she felt bad. This woman was just trying to be nice to her.

She opened her mouth to ask the group if they had learned anything useful about the aliens or had any ideas about escaping, but was cut off.

"So how are you doing with everything Jess?" Amy asked.

She looked at Amy with astonishment. Her mouth opened and closed a few times in a good imitation of a goldfish before she realized the woman genuinely seemed to want an answer to the question. So she blurted out the first thing that popped into her head.

"Uhhh, well I can't say I'm doing too good Amy, what with being abducted and raped by aliens and all. You understand I see," she said with sarcasm leaking into every syllable and waved at the obvious bulge of second trimester pregnancy that swelled under Amy's white dress.

The color drained from Any's face at the crude words.
Dammit, what is wrong with me?

This was not going as planned. She seemed fine until she was expected to talk, at which point her rancorous, bitchy shadow self apparently took over her mouth without warning.

Amy recovered and continued to play the part of Suzy Sympathy.

"Well darlin', no need to be so sour about it! It's true we've all been through a…tough time here, but that's no reason we can't be sociable. We girls have to stick together in situations like these."

Jess threw her head back and roared with bitter laughter.

Uh-oh. Shadow bitch did not like that at all.

Women from several of the surrounding groups turned to look at her in surprise.

"Sociable? *Sociable*?! Are you fucking kidding me? I mean, you must be joking. Situations like these? How many 'situations like these' have you encountered before, Amy? Been raped by aliens before, have you?"

She turned to some of the other woman standing in the group. "How about you? Or you? You?"

They blushed and mutely shook their heads as she turned on them respectively.

God, what is going on?

She didn't seem to have any control over her mouth at all. She'd gotten too used to saying whatever the hell she felt like with the aliens, and of course to herself.

Amy flushed indignantly.

"Well I didn't mean…I wasn't saying…"

She quickly cut off the woman's sputtering response. "All I want to know is how to get out of here. Does anyone here know anything at all about how to get the hell out of this place?!" Her voice rose to a shrill pitch by the time she finished the sentence.

More women trailed off from their conversations and craned their necks to look at her.

She railed at Amy and her little clique. "How can any of you stand around here fucking *socializing* after we've all been kidnapped and unwillingly impregnated by fucking aliens? I mean, you've all experienced the same thing right?"

Hmm, ok. Here's some Spartacus action. Roll with it Jess, keep it going.

A chorus of sheepishly muttered yeses sounded around her and renewed blushing broke out amongst them.

Amazing, these idiots aren't even talking about any of this. They just get together in this god forsaken room and gossip about who the hell knows what. Then they go back to their complete isolation with nary a smidge of effort towards escape.

She could not have been any more disgusted if she tried. She took a deep breath, summoning patience and trying to wrestle her filterless new shadow friend under control.

"That's what I thought. So has anyone, anyone at all, considered gathering any and all details about these assholes? Learning everything they can about what's really going on here and formulating some kind of escape plan?"

They all glanced around at each other in wide-eyed embarrassment.

"I'm taking your silence as a no. Fucking wonderful."

"Well there is no reason we can't all support each other." Amy tried again.

Jess sighed and rubbed her temples.

These women are already giving me a headache.

"I'm not against us supporting each other. That's fine, perfectly fucking lovely. But there's also no reason we can't try to rally together and figure out a way to escape."

"But we're in space," said a dark skinned, only slightly rounded brunette standing to Amy's right.

Amy inexplicably elbowed the woman and Jess gave her a fleeting frown. She'd be damned if she would let Abduction Barbie waylay her plan.

"How does anyone actually *know* we're in space though?" she demanded. "They could have just told all of us that to keep us from trying to escape. So they wouldn't have to put down a revolt."

Several of the women nodded contemplatively at that.

Ahh, progress.

Amy's eyes shifted around the room, as if she was trying to be as uninvolved as possible.

What is her deal anyways?

"It's every bit as possible we're in some warehouse or something, on Earth. And if we can figure out a way to get out of the building, we can find the nearest town, call the police and blow this whole operation wide open."

More nods. Amy just bit her lip.

"So how do we get out of the building?" the brunette asked with a hard glint in her eyes.

I think I'm gonna like this one. She seems feisty.

"Well, I don't know how to use the doors or where they even are for that matter, so that may be tricky. They don't seem to do anything but stand in front of them for a few seconds and they just…open. Has anyone else seen anything different?"

They all shook their heads. A couple of verbal no's sounded here and there.

"Ok, so as far as we know, you just have to-"

She was cut off by the ear shattering wail of klaxons.

Women immediately plastered themselves to any free space along the wall, or huddled on couches with their hands over their ears.

Jess's hands flew up to her ears and Amy and her group all fell to their knees, trying to shut out the bone jarring racket.

Jess looked down at Amy, who was shouting something at her. She tried to read her lips to figure out what she was saying, since she certainly couldn't hear her.

Then the door opened and four aliens stormed into the room. They fanned out in front of the entry with their guns pointed at the room at large. One of them headed straight for Jess.

Shit.

It grabbed her arm and hauled her out of the room, the rest of the aliens following. The alarm shut off just as the door closed behind her.

The alien holding her arm addressed her.

"You will not discuss or attempt escape, or you will be removed from the exercise room."

"Man fuck you! What do you expect?"

"If you continue to discuss or attempt escape you will lose your privileges."

"Privileges?! You call gossiping with a room full of fellow rape victims a fucking privilege?" she cried.

"An opportunity for exercise and mental stimulation is provided to you in exchange for your services. It is a privilege."

Jess gaped up at the alien as she was hustled down the corridor. She had to practically run to avoid her feet being simply dragged along behind her.

"Are you fucking kidding me??"

"I am not attempting to be humorous."

"Unbelievable," she muttered. After another minute of walking/jogging down the hall, the alien turned to the wall and it opened. It placed her in her room with one final admonition.

"If it happens again, the consequences will be more severe."

It exited the room.

The continued ringing in her ears made her a little light-headed.

She sank down into her corner and remembered what she thought she'd read on Amy's lips.

This is why we are sociable.

CHAPTER SEVEN

A week passed before she was escorted from her cell again. She was led into the bathroom and couldn't contain a sigh of relief. This time she lathered herself with the utmost haste until her skin and hair practically squeaked. She hadn't been clean in a month and vowed she would never under-appreciate the tiny shower in her apartment ever again. Or her own clothes for that matter. Or conditioner.

If they actually let me go, after.

She scrambled to put on the clean dress sitting on the bench, before her alien attendant returned. She didn't want to deal with that whole situation again. Once was humiliating enough.

No more peep shows for these assholes.

To her surprise, she wasn't immediately returned to her room.

Instead she was escorted through the maze of hallways into a coffin-like chamber where she couldn't extend her arms more than a handful of inches to either side. Luckily she wasn't claustrophobic, but she did get a little freaked out when the faintest hum began to permeate the space.

After a few minutes with nothing but the hum and her increasing heart rate to distract her from her entombment, the door opened.

"What the hell was that about Gazoo?" she demanded, glaring out from the tiny nook.

Nothing.

"Seriously? You put me in some closet for five minutes and you can't even tell me why? I'm a person, I have a right to know what's being done to me. And somewhere in your tiny fucking alien brains you must recognize that, or you wouldn't have given me that little speech when I was first brought here."

It seemed to glance down at her then and appeared to consider her request. After a long moment of silent stare-down it finally spoke.

"Your pregnancy is confirmed. The embryo has successfully implanted in your uterus."

Jess gaped at it for a moment, dumbfounded, before it grabbed her arm and began the march back to her cell.

She struggled not to regurgitate her breakfast as the horrifying confirmation sank in. Her stomach churned and she swallowed forcefully several times, trying to loosen the tightness in her throat. Her heart was racing even more than it was in the chamber and she broke out in a cold sweat.

Huh, this is familiar…funny how…

Before the thought was even complete, the burn of bile hit the back of her throat and she bent over to hurl. Her guard took a hasty step away from her, but she was pretty sure some of the vomit splattered into its robe.

Good.

Once the retching stopped, she straightened and wiped her mouth with the back of her hand to find the alien frowning slightly at her. At least she guessed it was a frown, she had yet to determine if it had actually had eyebrows. Or, you know, emotions.

"You should not be losing nutrients at this stage of pregnancy. It has also been noted you are underweight and too often, do not eat your meals. Along with the supplemental nutrition you receive in your water, you will be given increased food rations."

"Great, that's absolutely wonderful. So I can puke up or ignore extra food now. Wait, you put shit in my water?"

"An analysis of the water commonly consumed by humans revealed that it contains no additional nutrition. We have corrected this deficiency. You will continue to receive supplements tailored to your specific nutritional needs based upon the results of your scans."

"Huh, that's cool. I don't even have to take the prenatal horse pills. I hate taking pills." She paused.

What the hell am I saying? Who gives a shit if this goddamned alien baby is healthy or not? Jesus am I already developing Stockholm syndrome here?? Yeah, that is so not gonna happen.

In response, it simply grabbed her arm and resumed the march back to her cell. Once there, she mulled over her options of things to think about.

Hmm, confirmation of the alien life form growing inside me, or the running favorite this week, last week's dramatic reintroduction into 'society'.

She shuddered and her now empty stomach rumbled dangerously in answer, as if warning that while it contained no food it would be happy to produce more bile for her to puke up - if need be.

Society it is then.

So she ruminated on her strange reaction to Amy and company. She spent hours reviewing everything that had happened in the 'exercise room', in anticipation of the next time she'd be allowed back in. That is, if they would even talk to her again. She really wouldn't blame them if they didn't.

But that didn't mean she wasn't going to try to work out another escape plan, either. Except this time she would use metaphorical language or some kind of code or…something. She'd figure it out, it's not like she lacked time to think about it.

I'll be dammed if I'm going to just give up because of the threat of no play time. Seriously, eff that.

In the meantime though, might as well shrink herself a bit. Her reaction to the women, even after the extended period of isolation, was out of character. Thanks to her job in retail, she was quite used to burying her personal opinion and carrying on. But given the circumstances she was willing to cut herself some slack. She had absolutely no outlet for her feelings in this place. And even though those women had gone through the exact same thing she had, she'd just lost it. Honestly the fact that they had experienced the same trauma only seemed to make her angrier.

The soul sucking tedium of continual solitary confinement, combined with the shock of realizing she was one of many women these aliens viewed as nothing more than a commodity, had shredded any remnants of her already precarious self-control. She probably had some PTSD going on, except this wasn't post anything yet so she didn't exactly know what to call it.

And now, on top of all that, she also felt like a complete fool - having shoved her foot so far into her mouth she was now choking on it. She was embarrassed.

The fact that her outbursts had seemed beyond her ability to manage was disturbing to her. She had always been proud of her self-control, but ever since she woke up in this fucking room, all hints of restraint had apparently evaporated.

Usually only people that knew her really well, relatively speaking, ever got so much as a glimpse of foul-mouthed, rebellious inner Jess. And even then she toned it way down. On the surface, she played by all the rules and as a result people generally got along well with her. It was all part of her strategy to keep people at a distance, and still make herself likeable and relatable to anyone.

She had a lot of friends and acquaintances but no one ever got to see inside her, to truly know her mind. That's how she'd always wanted it. Though if someone had asked her why, she wasn't entirely certain she could answer the question. She'd been in the habit of strict self-monitoring as long as she could remember and now she wasn't sure what to do with this new person evading her previously strong discipline.

She had always been the safe bet, the predictable one. Most people assumed she was a nice, polite, impeccably groomed and generally fashionable young woman who was occasionally known to cut loose a little, but only a little. She had even resisted her rather compelling urge to get a couple of easily hidden tattoos, which she'd wanted to do for years now. She was usually the master of temperance.

But that regulation and self-control now seemed to be slipping, and she didn't like it one bit. She had just barely wrestled her mind and words in the right direction, well, kind of, after some serious effort.

Apparently being abducted and raped by aliens is a little much for even me to handle. Go figure.

So she tried to go a little easy on herself and move on. Not much point in continually flogging herself over it.

I'll just have to do breathing exercises or fucking...meditate or something.

She laughed out loud at that thought.

Right, meditation will fix all my problems.

So she had acted like a total asshole to those women. Rubbed their shared condition in their faces and made arrogant assumptions that she was better and stronger and smarter than any of them. Looked down on them for not acting like she might expect them to. People who actually knew what she was going through and could sympathize with her.

She would apologize, try to start over.

So she had been naïve to assume the aliens would let her get away with rallying the women together, pulling her Spartacus.

She would try the subtle approach.

What had she expected anyway? Of course the aliens wouldn't allow their brood mares to conveniently plot a jail break with each other. Of course they would threaten to remove the one thing that might keep her sane in this beyond crazy situation. And of course they wouldn't give two shits that she needed some hope of escape to avoid a total mental breakdown. These were the same assholes that casually provided everyone with Dial soap and Evian water, oblivious to the fact that seeing these things actually made the situation so much worse.

So there's that, I've got my next moves. Apology, subtle mutiny.

She waited patiently, not like there was any other option, to be taken back to the group room.

Time dragged on endlessly and she began to wonder if they ever *would* let her go back.

Two weeks passed and she was taken for another shower. So there was that little bit of excitement.

Woo fucking hoo. I get to bathe bi-monthly. Cheap bastards.

Another week passed after the shower.

At least she'd had plenty of time to refine her plans on how to best approach the obvious monitoring situation. Now all she'd been waiting on was the access.

When an alien finally came to her cell for another game of grab and go, after a month of 'time out', she yanked her arm back and informed it she didn't require assistance. She threw her chin up and swept out of the room, trying her hardest to exude dignity.

Of course she didn't know where she was going, so she had to wait for it to lead the way. She could only hope they were headed back to the group room because she didn't think she could handle any other surprises.

Jess almost skipped with anticipation as she walked down the hallways. She'd say they were familiar now, but she had yet to be able to make any sense out of where anything was because everything looked the same. Shortly, the alien performed its customary obscure door opening ritual and guided her into the room.

"Remember, you are not to discuss or attempt escape again or the consequences will be worse than last time."

"Fucking bite me E.T.," she muttered under her breath as the door closed.

CHAPTER EIGHT

This time, there was no staring around in awe, no stupor, or even much anxiety. She was prepared - or at least that's what she told herself.

She stopped just inside the door and looked around for Amy and her gang. They were gathered around a couple of couches in the far left corner of the room, some sitting and others standing.

Don't they ever actually walk around? Meh, who am I to judge?

She meandered her way casually over to the women.

"Hey guys. I…I wanted to apologize for last time. I was a complete ass, and I'm sorry. There was no reason for me to act that way towards any of you…and…I know that you were just trying to be nice Amy, so a special apology to you for my behavior. I guess I kind of snapped and that's unusual for me."

Amy waved away the apology with a smile.

"No worries sugar, we all go a little crazy here and you're new so you didn't know any better."

Some of the other women nodded or hummed their agreement and forgiveness with an "it's ok" or "that's understandable" here and there.

"Wow, really? That was easy, thanks."

"Sure, hon. Like I said before, us girls have to stick together in these kinds of situations."

Having exhausted her store of interest in niceties, she simply nodded and took a deep breath.

Well, time for Spartacus: Redux.

"So, I was wondering, how many of you have ever been through *Port*land?"

She gave Amy a hard, hopefully meaningful stare and treated the other women sitting and standing around in the group to the same look.

Amy narrowed her eyes and gave Jess an almost imperceptible nod, followed by a slight frown.

Huh, talk about mixed signals.

A few of the group just stared uncomprehendingly at her, but several of them got a speculative gleam in their eyes and nodded.

Good, I have definitely underestimated them.

The feisty brunette jumped head first in to her game.

"I've been a few times, and I'm pretty sure it's an easy city to love. In fact, I absolutely have plans on going again one day, if I can manage it."

Oh, this one was perfect and this would work, she knew it. It had to. The light of understanding slowly grew in the previously blank stares.

"Oh yeah? I've only seen it on TV before, but I would definitely go if I got the opportunity. I've heard great things about it. What would make it hard to manage?"

"Well, I think it's a little difficult to navigate, but getting there is the tricky part."

"I've heard that, I'm sorry I don't know your name…"

"Alexis."

"I've heard that, Alexis. Nice to meet you, by the way. So, what would you say is the tricky part of getting there?"

"Well, the surrounding area is pretty well-populated and the exits aren't well-marked, to start."

"Hmm, that does sound a little tricky. What would your advice be on how to circumvent those two issues?"

"I'd say one thing that escapes most people's notice is the fact that while the surrounding area is well-policed and seems violent on the surface, the cops there won't really shoot you these days. So that's one less thing to worry about."

She placed her hand on her the slight bulge of her relatively early pregnancy.

"Oh really? I've wondered about that a few times myself. It seemed to be the case on the news, but it's always good to get a second opinion."

"Yeah I'm pretty sure they want to avoid the locals getting hurt."

"That makes sense."

"It does when you think about it."

They smiled broadly at each other.

Several other women joined in with smiles of their own as pleasure at the flow of understanding spread around the group.

If these fuckers won't actually shoot us now that we're pregnant, things are looking better and better for an escape attempt.

"I've noticed it seems to be a pretty cosmopolitan city all in all, with a pretty diverse population. Did you experience any difficulties communicating with people there?"

Jess wondered how far this little charade would get before the aliens caught on and brought down the hammer.

Alexis nodded.

"It is pretty diverse and communication would occasionally be an issue, but I did also find plenty of people to talk to."

"Well, that's a relief. I wouldn't want to get there and find only a small group of people to talk to - kinda defeats the purpose. Do they also know about what a marshmallow big brother is?"

"I was definitely not the only one who's noticed it, for sure. While I was there, I noticed a couple incidences of difficulties they had in controlling the population because of their reluctance to actually shoot anyone."

"So it would seem that we're back to the tricky navigation issue."

Alexis nodded again.

"Yeah. Most of the buildings all look the same, so there are really no landmarks to guide you."

"That is definitely a problem. But honestly, in light of everything else you're telling me, it still sounds worth a trip."

"Oh it's definitely worth a trip. I think once you find the right exit and it's somehow not blocked off, it's not all that hard to find your way in. Hey listen, do you guys want to walk around? I'd like to stretch my legs a little."

Alexis got up off the couch and the others followed suit. She headed away from where the door was.

A crafty one, our Alexis.

They sedately walked around the room once and then oh so casually set up near the door to continue the conversation.

Alexis inclined her head towards the door, with a direct stare at Jess. She took it as her cue to position herself closest to the door, so she wormed her way over to it. Once the others realized what she was doing, they clustered around her by unspoken agreement.

Now that she was placed, she had no idea how to continue their cover in light of what was about to be some obviously strange behavior. There'd be no other reason for her to just stand there, facing the wall.

Well, this isn't going to happen by just thinking about it.

She whipped around and stepped towards the door and waited.

And waited.

Every muscle in her body was tense, straining, willing the door to open.

Goddammit this isn't working. We can't open the doors. Why? How the hell do they open?

They had to be coded to only work for the aliens, in some way that wasn't readily observable.

She waved her hands in front of the door, hoping there was some sort of sensor to trip.

The women around her fidgeted and they were all waiting for the ear shattering sirens to sound at any second. Obviously, it took a few minutes for the aliens to organize once they knew something was up.

She decided that this might be their only shot, with everyone being on the same page and advantageously placed for action. She turned and addressed the group in a low, urgent tone.

"When they come in, I'm going to attack the first one through the door. If anyone else has any hope of escape, this will probably be our only opportunity. After I take out the first one, I'm running for it. They're quick but if we ambush them together and get a head start, we might have a chance. If we can get past this area where all the doors are obviously coded to ignore us, we might be able to find a way out. Who's with m-"

Her rushed little speech was cut off by the wail of the alarm. She widened her eyes at the group and nodded to the door, hoping the words she'd been able to get out were enough. Then she whirled back around to the door to await the aliens. She didn't wait long.

Though it felt like an eternity due to resisting the urge to cover her ears, mere seconds passed before the door slid open to reveal an alien standing in the passage with a gun pointed directly at her.

Jess kicked out at the gun, sending it flying out of its hand. She couldn't reach its face so she lowered her head and shoulders and charged it like a linebacker, using a brief crouch to drive into it.

Though she didn't have much momentum, the alien was so surprised and unprepared that it stumbled back into its fellows lined up behind it and they started going down like dominos. Jess toppled down along with it but used the position to her advantage. She smashed her fist into its face a few times with a grin of sadistic pleasure and sprung off it. Then she stumbled over another alien a couple steps away but managed to right herself before she fell completely and took off down the hall.

She raced away from the pile-up and risked a glance backwards. Alexis was right behind her as were five other women. The alien she had taken great pleasure in punching was trying to climb to its feet amidst the flow of women escaping the exercise room. Amy and another woman were still struggling with two of the aliens. A third alien was occupied with trying to keep hold of the women in its grasp. Others were ganging up on alien that was trying to block the doorway, rather unsuccessfully, as the women that weren't committed to beating the shit out of it were still trickling out of the room. That one went down as she turned back to focus on where she was going.

Chaos. Glorious chaos.

A smile once again spread across her face as she tore down the hall and turned a corner.

This might actually work. Those fuckers didn't know what hit them. Goes to show what you know about women, assholes.

Her legs pumped furiously as the distance between them and the scene they left behind grew at a satisfying rate. The sound of the sirens faded away.

They continued their sprint through the rat maze of steel, turning and twisting their way through endless, indistinguishable hallways. She had no way to know if they were simply running around in circles or not.

Some of the women began to fall behind, and after two months of literally no cardio, she was more than a little winded herself. They all eventually slowed down to a jog, then a walk, and finally to a complete stop.

Jess bent over and looked up at the six other women who were all doing the same thing.

"Now what?" Alexis wheezed.

"Ok. We have to….just keep….moving. We can't…..let…..let them find us." Jess huffed back.

"But how do we get out of here?"

Jess held up her a finger and took several deep, slow breaths to steady her breathing and heart rates.

"We keep moving. It's gonna be hard for them to find us if we don't stay in one place. There has to be an open passage to the rest of the building somewhere. If not then…we can always attack anyone coming through an open door and continue on. It's worked so far. They really won't shoot us, and if we have surprise on our side, we just might make it all the way out."

The others merely nodded, most of them still too winded to offer much feedback on her plan. They took off again at a brisk jog.

Unsurprisingly, all the women with her seemed to be in fairly early stages of pregnancy. She couldn't imagine the women with larger bellies would have made it too far.

They kept going for about ten minutes before a couple of the women came to a halt, bringing the rest of the group to a stop as well.

"This isn't going to work, there is no way out of here," complained a red headed women with a similar build to hers.

"We can't get through any of these doors, or even tell where they are, so how are we supposed to get out?" asked a short, raven haired woman with startling green eyes and a slightly rounded stomach.

"Now we're all going to get in trouble," said a statuesque black woman with close cropped hair. She looked to be at the end of her first trimester.

Hm, that's pretty impressive.

"Well we've come this far, it's a waste of time to complain about it now," said a mid-height, curvaceous black woman with long purple locs. As far as Jess could tell, she wasn't showing much.

The only other member of their little rebel group- a small woman with olive toned skin- said nothing. She was too busy looking around nervously, or maybe she didn't speak English. She looked to be early mid-trimester. How she had kept up with everyone else was beyond her.

Whatever, girl power.

"Exactly. We've just got to keep trying," Alexis asserted.

Stole the words right from my mouth.

"She's right, let's just keep going," Jess sighed.

They continued to wander the corridors, alternately jogging and fast walking. The frustration of the group steadily rose until it was almost palpable. The red head stopped again and the rest of the group followed suit.

Jess turned towards the whiney woman a give her a piece of her mind. As she turned however, over the shoulder of the red head, she saw a group of five aliens rounding the corner at the furthest end of the corridor.

Everything from that point seemed to happen in slow motion.

She turned to run the other direction and the rest of the women noticed their most recent problem. Alexis happened to be behind her, so when they turned she was in the front. They ran a ways down the hall before, incredibly, a portion of the steel wall ahead of them and to the right rippled and began to flow out like quicksilver. It quickly filled out to form a whole new portion of wall that slid across the hall to block their escape route.

What the actual fuck?? she thought, before noticing that Alexis wasn't slowing down.

Maybe she thought she could beat the goddamned magical wall stretching across the hallway. Somehow, the material of the walls was mutable but also solid - physics be damned. And Alexis wouldn't make it through.

"Stop, Alexis! *Stop*!" Jess screamed as she ran after her. "ALEXIS!"

Alexis slammed at full speed into the new wall just as it connected with the other side, and bounced off.

Jess skidded to a stop next to her. Blood was trickling from her shattered nose and mouth and a bright red stain was blooming on the dress from between her legs. Her front teeth were completely missing and several other teeth were cracked and jagged.

"No. No. Alexis, no," Jess whispered hollowly.

She knelt down next to the unconscious woman and her hands flittered over her as if she could fix her by will alone.

The blood between her legs was gushing now, soaking the whole lower portion of her dress. Jess was rapidly drenched by the growing puddle.

"I'm sorry, Alexis. I'm sorry, I'm so sorry. You'll be ok, you'll be ok, you'll be fine," she muttered.

She glanced up to see the aliens were now halfway down the hall. As they got closer her ears began to ring and she lost almost all muscle coordination.

Jess tried to open her mouth to warn to the rest of the women, but found she couldn't speak or even open her mouth. In fact, every molecule of her body seemed to weigh a ton and she found herself inexplicably laying down on the floor.

She saw the aliens approach and two of them lifted Alexis from the floor and carried her away. The rest of the women were also on the floor.

What the hell is going on here? she thought, before she passed out completely.

CHAPTER NINE

When Jess awoke she was back in her cell, on the gurney.

She scrambled off it and looked down to find she was still wearing the blood soaked dress.

God, what the hell happened back there? That was...really fucked up. I wonder what they did with Alexis. I hope she's going to be ok. She seemed pretty messed up.

Following that thought, she was immediately consumed with guilt as she remembered everything that happened.

Shit, was this my fault?

Something had obviously happened with Alexis' pregnancy when she hit that wall. And she felt responsible.

She wasn't too concerned about the loss of one of these goddamn alien rape babies. Maybe that made her a psychopath, oh well. But she was worried about Alexis. Her only real ally in this whole messed up situation. Someone she actually liked.

She had encouraged this, made it happen. So she was responsible for the events that transpired. She'd been the ringleader and she had messed up. Big time. And someone had gotten hurt because of her.

Will they even tell me if she's going to be alright? And what the ever living hell was up with that wall? Or for that matter, the paralysis that seemed to affect everyone when the aliens caught up with us.

Fucking aliens. Who knows what kind of weird shit they're able to do. Clearly they aren't as benign as they try to seem.

Her thoughts were interrupted by the hiss of the door and not one but two aliens stepped into her cell.

"How's Alexis? Is she going to be ok?"

"We are simply here to inform you, you will be confined to this room for the foreseeable future. You have abused the privileges extended to you."

"Yeah fine, whatever. How is Alexis?"

"You will not be permitted to leave your room until you can prove you will no longer attempt to escape."

"Sure, ok geniuses, how am I supposed to do that if I'm confined to this room?"

The speaker seemed taken aback by the question and looked over at its companion. They stared at each other in silence for several long moments.

"Worm Guys, hellooo? I'm still here, do you want to go get a room or something? I said, how am I supposed to prove I won't escape while I'm stuck in this room?"

In response they turned and left.

"Jesus *Christ* they are thick," she asserted to the room.

Hours passed before one of them returned with a clean dress, which it placed on the floor then backed out of the room without a word.

She changed into the clean garment and stared at the blood soaked dress crumpled in front of the door. Thoughts whirled in her head, her mind refused to settle onto any one thing.

Several more hours came and went before her dinner tray arrived. Despite everything, she did manage to get down some of the food.

Time stretched endlessly before her.

Two months passed in complete isolation.

All she had to look forward to was the arrival of her food. She began to draw out eating as long as she could as a way to occupy herself.

She figured out a couple of valuable tricks to help her keep her sanity, or at least try to.

Like tearing off bits of her hem to stuff into her ears when the sound of her own breathing became too much for her to cope with.

She perfected the art of the self pep-talk.

She slept. Constantly.

She sang all the songs she could remember.

She came up with new and, she thought, innovative insults to try on the aliens when they came to her cell.

She counted out the two week periods, when she knew she would get a shower. The day before a scheduled shower, she would almost completely shred apart her white dress for decoration material for her cell.

By the end of two months she had what she considered a decent collection of bows, knots, 'streamers' and loops.

She had even started working on making a little doll that she talked to.

One thing she didn't do at this point, was analyze anything she did too closely.

She hated to admit it, but the 'exercise room' had begun to seem more and more like a privilege after all. As much as she had initially scorned the assertion that is was 'a courtesy', it sounded pretty damn appealing right about now. On the other hand, the false hope she'd given herself based on the presence of other people had led her to where she was now.

And Alexis, she didn't know what had actually happened to her. So after a while she decided it wasn't the best idea to think about that whole…situation.

Since she would somehow have to 'prove' she wouldn't try to escape again, she decided it would be in her best interest to just act as docile as she possibly could. With that plan in mind, she waited for her next opportunity to prove what a biddable little uterus she could be.

She figured the first time she'd been slapped with one month of isolation, so this time would probably be two. Those two months had passed, so she was due to go back to the group room any day now.

The last month had been the hardest.

She'd struggled - not all that successfully - against a deep depression. She couldn't imagine anyone who had been in complete isolation for two months would be faring any better than she was, but it wasn't exactly comforting to know that.

She had become increasingly worried about her sanity, despite her resolution to not analyze her behavior.

One night she'd been awoken by the strangest sensation of comfort and contentment, the likes of which she hadn't felt since she'd been here. Or ever really, for that matter.

Occasionally, random, amorphous thoughts and images would flash through her mind. Before she could even decide what they were, they were gone.

Reverberating, muffled sounds began to startle her in the endless, still moments that made up her days.

Despite her general distaste - or outright loathing - for the life inside her, she talked to it as a way to ignore her apprehension over the hallucinations.

She poured out her grief, loneliness, despair, fear and anger to the only 'real' company she had. That it was the *cause* of these feelings was something she avoided thinking about too much.

She didn't know what to make of the sounds and images that continued to manifest in her mind with increasing regularity, but she feared she was experiencing a mental breakdown. She began to dread the moments when this would happen and her heart raced until she thought she would pass out from the accompanying dizziness.

She tried to tell her guards about it, but never received a single reply. They didn't seem to care in the least.

However, a couple weeks later she was taken to the scanning chamber again. She endured it with a little more patience this time, anxious to hear the results. That is, if she could actually get them to tell her what they were.

This was made all the more difficult by the fact that she was quite a bit larger than she would have guessed she'd be, at almost four and a half months pregnant. The scanning chamber was getting damned tight.

She waited for the door to slide open and happily squeezed herself out.

"So what's going on Krang, am I going crazy?"

It looked at her with its blank eyes and took its sweet time answering, while she practically vibrated with anxiety.

"There is some increased brain activity in the epithalamus region of your brain."

"Okaay, what does that mean?"

"It is not of concern. You are in good general health and it's not effecting your pregnancy."

"Wow, ok. That's about as helpful as…"

She struggled to come up with a good sarcastic response, but was too distracted to give it much effort.

"That's not helpful," she ended lamely.

"Your fetus is developing well and is healthy. It is a male."

Her jaw dropped open and she gaped at the alien for a few long moments. Then, its patience for dealing with her clearly gone, it grabbed her arm and marched her back to her cell.

She returned to her corner and sat down heavily, stunned by the news she had just been given. Not that she'd asked for it. Three simple words.

It's a boy.

Knowing the baby's sex made it real in a way it hadn't been before. In a way she hadn't *wanted* it to be. Sure, she talked to it. But somehow, it was still unreal. Still an 'it'.

Not anymore. Now, she would be giving birth to a boy. A son, she would have a son.

A half alien son. Jesus. That she would never see.

Did she *want* to, even if she could? She didn't know the answer to that.

Before she could continue with that delightful train of thought however, the word 'boy' echoed through her head with a sensation equivalent to a huge gong going off right next to both her ears.

She curled into a ball in the corner and clutched her head, teeth grinding together.

"Ahhh. What is going on here?!" she cried.

The word kept repeating, along with the jarring mental percussion. Her scalp prickled and her eyes watered as the pain became almost intolerable. A wave of nausea rolled over her and her skin crawled.

Well this is it, this is my complete mental breakdown.

She squeezed her head, desperately willing the pain away. She didn't know what kind of 'episode' she was having, but it needed to end. Like yesterday.

"Boy! Boy! Yesss, boy! Fucking boy! So what?!" she shouted, hoping if she replied to the question she was apparently asking herself, it would somehow magically stop.

And it did.

She uncurled herself from where she'd ended up on the floor and sat up, panting.

"What. The. Hell. Was that?" she grated through her teeth, still clutching her head. "God, that was horrible."

An overwhelming feeling of regret and sadness washed over her. It built until she could barely move. She moaned despondently.

"C'monnnn man. I can't…What the hell is going on? Stop!"

And it did.

"Ok. That's it. I've had about enough of this."

She stood up and pounded on the door so one of the guards would come to see what was going on. At which point she would demand another scan.

There had to be something wrong with her brain and she needed medical attention. Freaking immediately. She probably had some kind of brain tumor they hadn't told her about.

The door hissed open and she took a step back.

An alien stepped into her cell.

"You require attention?"

"Yeah I require attention. I'm having…"

She paused, at a loss for words to describe what had happened.

"There is…something wrong with my brain," she finally blurted. "I am having hallucinations, pain and hearing, you know, like a voice in my head. I probably need medication or…something. I need to be scanned again."

"You were just scanned. There is no cause for concern."

"Well I *am* freaking concerned here! This is not normal!"

"What is not normal?"

"Jesus," she said, rubbing her eyes. "Haven't you heard a word I said? Hallucinations, hearing a voice, sudden excruciating pain in my head? *Not normal*."

"Your scan indicated increased brain activity in the epithalamus region of your brain."

"No shit Sherlock," she muttered under her breath, then sighed with the utmost contempt. "Yes, I am aware of that. But right after the scan, all…this started happening so maybe you missed something."

"Our technology is far more advanced than anything you are accustomed to. It did not miss anything."

She just gaped at the hardheaded, obstinate alien. She couldn't be sure of course, but it almost seemed *pleased* with itself. Apparently superiority complexes weren't an exclusively human thing.

"Yeah, everyone thinks their technology is perfect, until it isn't. It's not *impossible* that it missed something. Or that you don't know as much about human anatomy as you thought."

"We spent twenty five Earth years studying human anatomy, we are-"

"Look, are you going to rescan me or not?"

In response, the alien's face became even more blank - if that were possible - and it stared off into the middle distance over her shoulder. At least she thought it did. She still couldn't tell exactly where their vision was directed half the time.

After a few very long minutes, the alien appeared to direct its attention to her once more.

"An additional scan will not be necessary."

"What! Why not? You can't just…seriously?" she sputtered.

The alien turned and left the room and the door hissed shut behind it

"Holy shit I hate these guys. Never thought I'd say this, but I miss the American health care system."

She sank dispiritedly back into the corner.

CHAPTER TEN

Luckily, the next couple weeks passed without any more crippling mental attacks. But she kept experiencing the same subtle hallucinations, which continued to worry her. As it didn't seem there was anything to be done about it, she tried to avoid thinking about what could be happening to her.

Then, she was escorted from her cell again.

She was a month overdue according to her calendar, but the aliens obviously weren't interested in *her* sense of justice. All in all, she had been decently distracted by her mental state, and talking to her…son.

A door hissed open onto the group room and she heaved a massive sigh of relief.

She wandered around the group room and looked for any sign of Alexis.

She figured Amy was long gone by now. The first time they'd met, Amy had already been quite pregnant.

It was exceedingly strange to think that Amy was now back at home, back to…whatever kind of life she'd been taken from. She had managed to avoid thinking about either of them for the last two months. But now - being back in contact with people - it rose to the forefront of her mind again.

After looking around, and asking everyone she encountered if they had seen Alexis, or knew how she was doing, Jess was utterly discouraged. The reactions she received ranged from expressionless stares to what sounded like a lot of swearing in multiple languages.

She was totally shunned, even by those who spoke English. And if looks could kill, she'd have been long dead.

She hadn't taken enough notice of the other women in Amy's little group, aside from Alexis, to recognize any of them now.

She settled onto a couch with a loud sigh of frustration.

Well, now what?

She had pretty much given up hope of escape at this point. Movement had become pretty awkward and if her calendar was in any way accurate, she only had a little over four more months of this hell left to go. But it would seem very long indeed if no one would even talk to her.

"Good thing your mother isn't going to be sticking around much longer, little alien dude, because she is not very popular," she murmured to her stomach with a pat. She was feeling generous towards him today for some reason.

"Mother?" asked a quavering voice.

She started and looked around for the speaker.

Great, *now* what? Had she offended someone by using the word mother?

There was a woman standing close enough to have been the culprit. But by the time Jess opened her mouth to ask, the woman had looked over at her, shook her head and scurried away as fast as she could.

"Okaay then," she said with another sigh.

"MOTHER?" the voice asked again, louder.

"Jesus Christ!" she yelped and flew off the couch, stomach notwithstanding.

She continued to get dirty looks from the women within hearing range of her. Not that she'd noticed. Nope, definitely not.

Jess stood there for a moment, as confusion peaked to frustration. She watched the women milling all around her, simultaneously surrounded yet isolated.

The hairs on the back of her neck stood at attention as a thought she had been avoiding since the bizarre incident she'd termed "the attack" came to the forefront of her mind.

Maybe it's the baby.

Yeah right, it's the baby. The alien baby…

She gave a little chuckle out loud, just to relieve the tension building in her muscles. Maybe she *was* crazy after all. There was no way. Telepathy was a fairy tale, a myth. Ridiculous.

It would explain the 'magical wall' Alexis ran into…

God, that's right. It totally would.

But for crying out loud it sounded so irrational, even in her head. Then again, what else did she have to do except entertain outlandish ideas? She was already in probably the craziest situation she'd ever heard of, let alone been in, so why not?

Ok, so let's entertain…

They could have some kind of telepathic link into a control system for whatever the hell kind of metal they were using. And there was the whole stupor thing that every one of the women fell into. For that matter, it would also account for a good deal of their behavior. The strange pauses, the apparently empty stares, their seeming reluctance to explain anything. Out loud. Maybe they were talking to each other, telepathically.

It would definitely explain 'the attack'. Her baby. Trying to talk to her. Of course it, he, didn't know *how* to talk, so he had done the best he could to get her attention. He was learning to talk. In her head. Loudly.

Could this get any weirder?

As if she wasn't already carrying a forced alien baby, now it was friggin' telepathic too?

But then, why didn't they just communicate telepathically with the women? Maybe they could only link with some women? Hmm, possible. So it might be a good idea to ask around to see if she could find any other women experiencing the same thing as her.

Eventually, she found an English speaking group and edged towards it. She tried to maintain a discreet distance so she could get a feel for the crowd before they realized she was eavesdropping. Soon enough however, one of the women noticed her.

"What do you want, trouble maker?" asked a brunette with a sour look on her face.

She tried to look as innocent as possible.

"Who, me? I don't want anything, just walking around."

She added a nonchalant shrug for good measure.

"Sure," she replied flatly. "Why don't you go away? We're not interested in being part of another one of your pathetic escape attempts."

"Oh, no I'm not trying to start another escape attempt. Learned my lesson there. But say, have any of you noticed anything weird or unusual since you've been here? Since becoming pregnant? Like hearing voices or… experiencing any kind of mental attack?" she finished lamely.

Man, that sounded incredibly silly.

The brunette flipped her hair and laughed.

"God, you really are crazy aren't you?"

Several other women joined in the laughter. Jess shifted uncomfortably, then clenched her jaw.

Screw this, she thought and stormed off. The sound of laughter trailed behind her as she walked away to find another group to make a fool of herself in front of.

Over the course of the next month she asked at least another fifty women the same general question. There never really seemed to be a way to ask that didn't make her sound as crazy as she felt.

Some laughed, some gave her pitying glances, and some seemed angry at being asked to interact with her at all. Not a single one gave an affirmative reply.

She had tried to communicate telepathically with the aliens, to no avail. Not once did she get the slightest inclination she was succeeding on any level. She began to think she *was* just losing her mind, experiencing a psychotic break after all.

Despite all this, she continued to talk to her baby. Hell, if she was going insane, she might as well make the most of it. So she began to converse with him in earnest and attempted to teach him as much as she could about herself. She *was* his mother. Half of him was from her, human. And it certainly gave her something to do.

Within a few days, the baby - or the hallucination, depending on how she viewed it day to day - had learned a lot of basic words. She wasn't sure if that confirmed it as a delusion or not. This was her first alien baby, after all. Maybe they were much more intelligent than she had previously realized.

After she exhausted the topic of herself, she moved on to teaching it about Earth and its societies.

After two weeks, she felt he had a pretty strong grasp of English and everything she knew about world religions and governments. Which admittedly wasn't much, but she was surprised by how much she *did* know.

Along the way, she tried to impart the sum of her wisdom about human relationships and social customs. This led her to tell him about her family, friends, and the life she had on Earth.

Two more weeks passed companionably conversing with her…son. She was amazed by the lightning speed of his learning capabilities.

It was hard to keep thinking of the baby as a fetus, as just an alien, though he was. He had a personality, his own mind. He…loved her. And he had to be the most unique being on this entire ship.

She began to think, he could be different. She would teach him how wrong this 'program' was. Maybe he could be the one to change things. Her little rebel, her ace in the hole.

After only a month he had gained the general speech abilities of an early toddler. She was blown away by his comprehension skills.

Until one day, he asked her an impossible question.

"Can I stay with you when I'm born?"

CHAPTER ELEVEN

She was utterly flabbergasted, floored, speechless. And she didn't have an answer.

At some point, while she hadn't really been paying attention, she'd begun to have a distinctly maternal feeling towards her child. Despite the horrifying way he had been made, she had begun to love him.

Whatever the hell he might actually look like when he was born, he was half hers, carrying her genes. And definitely taking on parts of her personality. She garnered quite a bit of amusement from teaching him every swear word she knew.

He persisted in questioning her about coming with her back to Earth when he was born. She'd tried telling him it wasn't going to happen, she would be sent back to Earth - alone - after giving birth to him.

He didn't seem to find this answer acceptable no matter how many times she gave it. So ultimately, she decided to confront one of her jailers with her baby's request.

"Hey Jabba, got a dilemma for you."

After starting at her vacantly for the space of several awkward heartbeats, it answered.

"Please elaborate, I do not understand your statement."

"Thought you'd never ask. I've been talking to my baby, and he says he wants to live with me when he's born."

The the most rewarding look of confusion, incredulity and disbelief passed over its face, followed instantaneously by a return to its customary blank slate. But she'd seen it, what passed for brows furrowed, thin lips became even thinner, and its eyes widened the merest fraction. And it had been sweet indeed.

Bet they'd never heard this before.

"How *exactly* has your fetus said anything to you?" it recovered quickly to ask, with an air of condescension.

"Um, telepathically genius, how you all communicate."

It's 'brows' lowered again.

How delightful.

A huge grin spread over her face. Oh, this was too fun.

She heard the baby giggle internally and the grin spread even wider.

Funny mommy.

The alien didn't exactly sputter, but it was obviously at a complete loss for a response, so she attempted to leverage its uncertainty.

"I'm fairly positive that you've never had this request before, so your hesitation is understandable. However, my baby *can* communicate with me and has expressed that he wishes to remain with me, on Earth, after his birth. While you might not give a shit what any of your *victims* want, this baby is one of you, more or less. Obviously I have no idea how your society handles things like personal liberty or conflict resolution, or…well, anything really, but... there it is."

The aliens' gaze landed on her now sizeable belly and gave it what appeared to be an intense look, and then looked between her belly and her face several times with the same concentrated stare. As if it was trying to willfully extract the truth with its eyes alone.

She didn't think she had ever seen such personal interest from any of them before. Come to find out, it was not pleasant. She definitely preferred the impersonal, detached manner in which they typically interacted with her.

Then a sudden, horrifying thought took root.

What if this one is the baby's father?

She shuddered.

The scrutiny stretched for several seconds before she couldn't take the suspense or her own thoughts anymore.

"What the hell are you doing?" she blurted.

She didn't think she could stand knowing if this one was the father or not, so she didn't ask. Not that it would matter, because she still couldn't tell them apart but…

Mommy, what's father? she heard. *Is it like Dad?*

Not now little dude, she replied quickly.

The alien finally raised its eyes back to her face.

"I cannot communicate with the fetus."

"Well, that sucks for you, but I can. And I just told you what he wants. So what are you assholes gonna do about it?"

"I…do not know. I will take this information to the council."

"Yeah, take it to the council. Wait, shouldn't *I* be taking it to the council? I'm representing the baby, so shouldn't I be the one to address the council and state the baby's case, or whatever?"

In response, it stared off into space for several moments. Which she now knew meant it was communicating with whoever. The mysterious council probably.

"That will not yet be necessary."

"Well, if you just told them about it, they already know so I should just address the council myself righ-hey! What are you doing?!" she shouted as it abruptly turned and left the room without another word.

"Ugh!! *Freaking aliens!*" she exclaimed and stomped her foot impotently on the steel floor.

She paced as she waited for someone to come back and take her to the council. After about an hour she began to think no one was coming at all.

Then an hour stretched into a couple and her dinner tray arrived and was subsequently taken away.

Another couple hours passed.

Assholes. Am I ever going to get a chance to address this "council" at all??

Mommy, what is council?

Council in this case is a group of...people who will decide what happens with you when you're born.

But they can't hear me, only you?

Right. Which is a little strange when you think about it. They all have telepathy between themselves and you should have it too, but you can't hear each other. And I can, somehow.

You are special Mommy.

And you are sweet, little dude. Now I need to concentrate, so remember what we learned about our own separate spaces? Mommy needs some separate space.

Ok Mommy. I will try talking to the others more.

Alright buddy.

She felt a wave of love from her son - their mental equivalent of a hug - and with that she was 'alone' again. As alone as she ever got these days anyway.

She could always feel the shape of her son's consciousness on the periphery, within reach. Even when they were occupying their 'separate spaces', the comforting presence was always there, always accessible. Within the last month she'd come to rely on it much more than she cared to admit.

She was dozing off in her corner when the door hissed open.

"The council will see you now," one of the three aliens announced.

"Ok," she said groggily and sat up with a grunt. "Of course they'll see me *now*..." she trailed off, too nervous to apply herself to further berating them.

This was it, the big 'interview', her chance to change everything. Do or die. Well ok, not *die*, but certainly important.

She was a mother now, for whatever fucked up reason the universe had decided to make her one in this fashion. The urge to personally protect and care for this baby had at some point taken over, instinct apparently overriding everything else she was and had been feeling about the whole situation. Which was, admittedly, a lot. But she'd be damned if she wouldn't fight for this baby, knowing what she did about his wishes. Knowing what she did about who he already was as his own person. Nothing in her life had ever prepared her for something like this, any of this - how could it - so she would just do the best she could.

There was no way to predict what the aliens would decide, though she had pieced together a few things about them over the last almost seven months. Which wasn't much to go on. And she had never been all that interested in the intricacies of law, so she was basically going to be just winging it.

While it was true she had a lifetime of therapy in front of her to deal with the 'everything else', for now she was just going to focus on one thing at a time, and handle things as they were dealt to her.

After about five minutes of brisk walking, the aliens stopped in front of a wall. The accustomed hiss sounded, so softly she almost missed it.

The door opened into a room unlike anything she had seen so far on this damned…spaceship or whatever it was. The room was cavernous, dark and expansive with a curved ceiling. Far removed from the sterile, inhospitable feel of everything else she'd encountered - this room had soft lighting at the far edges of the space. She could just make out glints of metal, but the floors were covered with huge swaths of cloth - soft under her bare feet as they advanced into the room. There were no right angles anywhere, everything that reached her eyes appeared gentle, refined and muted.

The cognitive dissonance she experienced at this proof of depth and personality was unsettling. She didn't like it one bit. And if she hadn't already felt small and insignificant simply standing next to her freakishly tall alien guards, she felt positively miniscule now in this imposing space.

She swallowed hard.

Screw these aliens and their stupid, huge, tastefully appointed council room anyways. I'm not impressed.

She lifted her chin and marched forward with purpose.

They continued through the room until they reached a large metal dais, with three large, high backed steel chairs in the middle. Each chair was occupied.

These must be the head honchos of this entire goddamn abduction and rape operation, she thought with a sneer.

No, keep it cool Jess, you want something from them. Play nice.

As she got closer, she had to stifle a gasp of shock at the council's appearance. They looked almost entirely different from any of the aliens she had seen thus far. Their eyes were much larger with a silvery reptilian film that descended in place of eyelids, which the other aliens had, and the milky color was now almost opalescent with a strange marbled effect.

She gave a quick glance to the alien on her right to be sure. It looked back down at her and she shuddered.

Yep, definitely has eyelids, doesn't remind me of jewelry.

She couldn't be sure, but she squinted at their foreheads and thought she saw tiny, third vestigial eyes high up on the forehead, almost hidden by their markings. Only four fingers curled on the smooth arms of their chairs.

After being grabbed by them so many times, she had taken it for granted they all had five human-like fingers, though they were longer and bigger than the normal human hand. Instead of the small nose bulges she'd become used to, they had simple slits which flared and retracted with each breath.

That's not friggin distracting.

And they were bigger still than any alien she had encountered so far, even seated she guessed they were nine or ten feet tall. Their skin wasn't just patterned, but actually grooved with the markings, creating ridges and channels in their skin. And the skin itself had almost none of the beige tones with silver highlights of the others, instead being almost completely metallic with the merest tracing of dark, black-brown veining.

She swallowed again, trying to create moisture in a mouth suddenly gone dry.

Guess I've been seeing the watered down version.

The one in the middle spoke.

"We've been informed you have a telepathic link with your fetus. Is this true?"

"Fu-" She stopped herself just in time. "Yes," she answered instead. "It's true, and my son has informed me of his wish to be cared for by me, on Earth. He wants to experience a human life."

The middle alien scrutinized her intensely. After a few moments, it spoke again.

"I cannot communicate with your fetus. Or you."

She shrugged.

"I don't exactly know how this works. Some other…one of you, already confirmed that this child can only communicate telepathically with *me*. I don't know why, I don't know how. But that's the truth."

"We have no way to verify if what you say is truth or not," it replied.

Jess opened her mouth and immediately closed it again.

The Prawn has a point.

"No," she admitted through clenched teeth.

A few moments of silence followed as they all communicated with each other. She assumed.

She could feel her son's avid attention on the proceedings. She gave him a mental hug, then the alien in the middle focused its iridescent eyes back on her.

"Setting aside the fact that there is no way to verify you can indeed talk to your fetus, where do you propose to live with your child once it is born?"

She did a repeat performance of opening and closing her mouth.

Dammit, why didn't I think of this beforehand?

"Well. I imagine when I return to Earth I can…I'll move to the country. Where there will be no other people around to find out about him."

"So you propose a life of isolation for this child, apart from any societal contact? Away from his people"

"Uhh yeah. That's what he wants. I've explained to him the downside of such an arrangement. He says he would still prefer to live on Earth, as opposed to in this ship or whatever it is, and be obligated to be a part of your *operation*," she sneered. "Which is bullshit, I'll just add, and my son agrees. I will also point out that humans are also his *people*."

Dammit.

She clenched her jaw at the slip up, her tone had turned into pure venom. She hadn't planned on offending them in this little interview.

The lead alien looked taken aback, as it sat back abruptly in its chair.

Silence filled the room and she shifted on her feet. She still wasn't used to the added pregnancy weight. Or the lack of exercise. Or the fact that her baby was half alien.

The middle alien sat up again.

"We will consider your request," it said and the alien on her right grabbed her arm and led her out of the room.

Jess had a sudden strange feeling as an unwelcome thought she'd had before floated to the surface, while they walked out and back into the maze of hallways.

She steeled herself for the information she was about to ask for, and looked to the alien on the right.

"Are you…"

Her throat closed as if physically unwilling to perform the required task. She cleared her throat and tried again.

"Are you the father of this child?"

It looked down at her and its eyes trailed down to her stomach.

"Yes," he answered. "I've been in charge of your care since you arrived."

They stopped in front of the wall and the door opened to her room.

"Oh," she said, and walked into the room and slid down into the corner.

The door hissed shut.

CHAPTER TWELVE

Three days passed before she was escorted from her room. She avoided looking at the alien on her right. She still couldn't be totally sure, but had a feeling that this was the same one. The father.

Does it really matter?

At this point she didn't know if she was going to the shower, the group room, or the council again. She didn't see much point in asking. Her alien 'suitor' didn't like to answer questions.

As the door opened, she saw that it was the council's room.

This is it.

What do you think they'll say Mommy?

I don't know son. I may have to come up with a Plan B here...I don't think this proposal has a good chance of succeeding.

You'll figure it out Mommy. You're special.

They walked across the vast room and stopped before the dais.

The head alien leaned forward.

"We have given your request careful consideration. Our response to your request, however, is no."

"What!" she shouted. "Why not?"

"Can you ensure us that there will be no danger to your child on Earth? No chance of discovery?"

Godammit.

Jess clenched her fists.

"No," she bit out.

"Can you ensure that if he is discovered, he will not be seized by your government, subjected to invasive testing, and suffer the loss of his free movement?"

"No," she grated through her teeth.

"Can you assure us that if he is discovered, and with him our entire program, there will not be any risk to our entire populace?"

She jerked her head sharply to the side to indicate no.

Fuck this guy anyway!

"If your child was discovered and our program revealed to humans, would they support it?"

She'd had enough of this passive aggressive bullshit.

"Fuck no they wouldn't you asshole!" she shouted. "You're abducting and raping us, and forcing us to carry alien babies, what do you expect?!"

She was grabbed on both sides. Jess swiveled her head to the right and glared at the alien.

"Get your goddamn hands off me E.T."

She yanked her arms away from both of them and charged at the dais. She wasn't at her fastest, being hugely pregnant, but she was still pretty quick. At least she impressed herself.

The alien guards caught up with her just as she was about to jump onto the dais and pulled her back. As she was dragged backwards, she spit as hard as she could at 'the council', hitting the middle alien right in the chest.

Ha, at least I still have good aim.

However, all sense of gratification fled as the council leader stood up. He was every bit as tall as she'd guessed, and maybe then some. She would say almost eleven feet.

Her ears started to ring in a horrifyingly familiar way, reminiscent of the episode in the hallway. Only worse.

"Ffffuuuck….you…….guuuys…" she managed, before she blacked out.

She awoke who knew how many hours later, to wild kicking and movement in her belly.

Her son's voice came to her, distantly at first, then sharpening into focus.

Mommy, mommy wake up. What's wrong? Why won't you wake up?

She struggled to a sitting position and slid off the gurney.

Its ok son, I'm here. I'm alright.

What happened Mommy?

Well, as you might have heard, they said no. And I didn't react well. Neither did the council leader.

Are you ok Mommy?

Yeah I'm ok. I need another plan.

It took her the remainder of the week to come up with a Plan B. She decided to try a bluff.

She'd inform her guard, the father, that she would starve herself and the baby to death if they wouldn't let her go free with her baby. She didn't think he wouldn't like that at all and would push the council *for* her.

It was a risky plan, and she didn't want to actually endanger her child's life, but she couldn't think of anything better. At least not yet. It's not like she had much to bargain with.

So she would try this and see what happened. They would *have* to care about one of their own babies wouldn't they? Their precious *program*.

So at her next meal, she told him. She more than told him actually, she knocked the tray out of his hands so he would get the picture that she was serious.

He gave her a trademark blank stare, then looked off over her shoulder. Minutes passed in silence.

But then, amazingly, she noticed a facial expression she had never seen before. She couldn't be sure, but she thought it looked an awful lot like anger.

"What, what is it? What did they say?"

"I will take your ultimatum to the council personally," he replied.

Hmm, that's unusual. There's something going on here.

But it was beyond her to imagine what alien politics were like, so she tried to distract herself by talking to the baby.

You know, we need a name for you.
Yes! I would love any name you gave me Mommy!
Haa! Oh really? What about Bartholomew?
That sounds like a fine name...
I'm kidding, I would never name you that dear.

What about Justine, Mommy? After your Mommy?

She chuckled.

Well, that's a girl's name son. You're not a girl.

Oh.

What about….Alex? I had a good friend once, in high school named Alex. He was a great guy.

I like it Mommy. He tried it out. *Alex.*

Alex it is then, my boy.

Lunch came and went.

Then dinner.

Hours passed as she waited for the now welcome hiss of the door. Eventually, she got so tired she couldn't keep her eyes open any more and laid down.

What seemed like just minutes later, she woke slowly to find her captor standing there, staring silently down at her.

"Jesus Christ!' she shouted with a jerk and struggled to sit up.

The alien folded itself down to help her up. For once, she let him. They stood face to face silently for a few moments before she couldn't stand the tension anymore.

"So what's the verdict? Are they going to reconsider letting little junior here come home with me?" she said, rubbing her stomach.

"I regret to inform you that the council is not persuaded to action by your threat. They say that while the loss would be regrettable, they have not reconsidered their decision. Indeed you and this child are unique, so it would be most disappointing were you both to perish. But they will not put the entire program and all of our people at risk. It is a sound decision."

He looked away over her head for a moment before turning to leave.

"Marvin, wait!" she called. "Do you agree? Even though this is *your* child?"

The alien stopped but didn't turn around.

Maybe it doesn't matter, he probably has a ton of children.

"How many children *do* you have?" she asked as curiosity got the better of her.

The moment stretched until she thought he would just leave without answering.

"This is my first child," he said, and left.

CHAPTER THIRTEEN

It took her another two weeks to come up with her final plan. Another threat. This time, she had concocted one whopper of a story.

She was going to tell them that when they sent her back to Earth, she would contact the U.S. government and expose their whole horrid operation, their *program*. But more than that, she would be taken seriously. Because she wouldn't contact just anyone who would listen, uh-huh. *She* wouldn't be laughed at. She would tell the aliens about her 'connection' inside an experimental branch of the government, an agency with the ability to view her memories.

She would threaten to reveal them to the whole world, out them if they didn't comply with her demand to take Alex home to Earth with her. She was done screwing around.

It was irrelevant that it was an entirely hollow threat, they wouldn't know that. She had been brushing off her rusty, retail-actress skills in the group room. She thought she was at least as good as she had been when she first got here, if not better because now she wasn't scared shitless and confused about what was happening to her.

This would work. It *had* to work.

As she got closer to full term and the looming separation approached, Alex had become nearly catatonic at times because of anxiety about his birth. And as much as she tried to be calm, it was affecting her too. She was afraid of telling the aliens about Alex's alarming issue though, for fear they would make her have an immediate C-section or whatever.

To say they had become close would be an understatement. Motherhood had taken on a whole new level with a telepathic child. Not that she had anything to compare it to, but she couldn't imagine a mother had ever before had *quite* the same opportunity for a relationship like this with their child. And her time with him was running out.

As the door opened, she stood up took a deep breath, readying herself for the next confrontation.

The alien stood in the doorway. He stared at her silently for a few moments before putting her tray on the ground and sliding it towards her. He stood up and made to move back and she called out to him.

"Wait! I've got one more thing for you to take to your council."

He stepped into the room the slightest bit.

"You tell that goddamn council of yours, that if they don't let me take my baby with me when he's born, I will go to the U.S. government and tell them everything."

He stared at her. "We have monitored many women upon their return to Earth. This is a harmless threat. Your governments don't take your claims seriously."

"Well, normally I would agree with you there Conehead, however I have a connection to an experimental agency. You wanna know what's special about *this* agency? I'll tell you. They can view memories."

"We have thoroughly monitored Earth's governments and have found no sign of such an agency."

"Well looks like you missed something there genius. It's a new agency, and I have a friend who works in it. When I get back, I'm going to have him scan my memories and take the information to his supervisors. And your whole goddamn *program* will be blown wide open. What do you think of that?"

He just stared at her, so she kept going.

"He will record my memories, and play them for the entire department. No amount of…whatever kind of technology you use to hide yourself from us, will cut it this time. With the right kind of proof, which I'll provide, humans will go all out to not only eradicate your precious program, but also wipe your entire species out of fucking existence. You ask your council, is it really worth *one life* to risk *all* your people?" she ground out sarcastically, remembering their previous rejections.

"I will take your ultimatum to the council," he finally replied.

"Yeah, you do that."

He turned and left her alone again. Alex piped up.

Do you think this will work Mommy?

I don't know honey, but I've got to try.

I just want to be with you. I don't want them to take you away.

I don't want them to take you away either Alex. I'm doing the best I can to make sure that doesn't happen.

You're a good Mommy. You love me.

Yes I do Alex, very much my baby. I want to hold you and love you and take care of you, sweetie.

They gave each other mental hugs and settled in to wait for the council's response.

The day wore on, and nothing happened.

Jess paced across her small cell until lunch came. She ate and then paced some more.

Dinner came and went. Hours passed, until she fell asleep.

It has to be a good thing that it's taking so long, right? she thought upon waking the next day.

Alex didn't respond.

He must be asleep or something. Or he's in another damn catatonic state. This kind of stress cannot be good for him.

Another day passed.

Then another.

If she thought time stood still before, it was nothing compared to the flow of hours now.

About an hour after dinner a week later, the door opened again. Her extraterrestrial baby daddy - she presumed - stepped into the room.

"Follow me, the council is giving you an audience," he said.

As always, she had difficulty interpreting his mental state, but he didn't seem happy.

They twisted and turned through the hallways until they reached the council chamber again. Probably for the last time.

Good, I've had about enough of these fucking Daleks and their whole fucking program. I cannot wait to get home, preferably with Alex, and figure out a way to move to the middle of nowhere and just live in peace. My parents can help me out I'm sure.

They reached the dais.

"So what's it gonna be Borg? You guys ready for your big Earth debut, or are you gonna do the smart thing and just let me take my baby home?"

"Silence your incessant chatter, human."

Jeez, Thing is in a bad mood today.

"The council has reviewed your ultimatum thoroughly. We conducted an extensive investigation into the feasibility of your threat. According to our newest research, you are correct."

Holy shit, really??

"The U.S. government is currently running an experimental program with memory retention and remote viewing."

Oh…my god! This is going to work!

"So the council convened to address your request in light of this new information. However, the fact remains that allowing you to take this child to Earth is out of the question."

Uh oh.

"What do you mean it's out of the question?! I'll have my parents help me move out to the country and take care of the baby. He'll be happy, well taken care of and protected! It's what he wants! I don't know what kind of crack pot laws you fuckers have, but if you've studied our culture, you understand that we have a concept called free will. Which is respected and considered in all decision making processes. I-"

"Enough," the council leader cut her off. "We are aware of your ruling principles. They are interesting and we have taken the concept into deliberation of this…unique situation. Unfortunately, we cannot weigh the needs of one of our own against the needs of all of us."

Shit.

"So we, once again, regret to inform you that we are declining your offer. Since your threat has been deemed credible, we will remove the memories of your time here from your brain's cortex. We extend our sincerest apologies that we have to resort to such drastic measures to protect our program, but you leave us no other choice."

Jess paled. She struggled against the spinning sensation threatening to suck her into unconsciousness.

This can't be happening. What have I done? They can't be serious. Can they really do this? There's no way...

The council leader continued, oblivious to her internal distress.

"Ordinarily such action is unnecessary. Your females are not taken seriously, have no proof of what has happened to them and are easily discounted by your own society. In this case however, your return to Earth, in keeping with the threat you pose, will require more effort. We will have to erase all the memories you created here, those of your family and friends, and anyone else who was involved with your disappearance. Your work supervisor, the police and so on. We will also remove all physical traces of your pregnancy and heal any damage giving birth will cause. Fortunately for you, we have the technology to do all this - though we don't normally expend our resources in this manner. The only other alternative is what your species would call 'humane dispatch'."

Jess opened her mouth, but nothing came out.

"Unless you would prefer the latter?" he asked.

She shook her head wordlessly.

"It is settled then. You won't remember any of this, which makes you luckier than most of our program participants. Thank you for your contribution. Your unique child will be a welcome addition to our populace, I have no doubt."

Her guard grabbed her by the arm and led her back to her cell. She walked, once more, mechanically back to her room.

Unable to process everything that had happened in the council room, she moved in a daze.

The alien ushered her into the room.

"I'm sorry," he said, before the door closed with a hiss.

CHAPTER FOURTEEN

After the disaster in the council's chamber, a week passed. A week in which Jess could hardly move, barely ate anything, and declined to go to the group room.

Then, sometime after the breakfast that marked her eight month in this living hell, she started feeling pain and what she assumed were contractions beginning in her distended belly. She remained in denial for the next few hours as they got increasingly worse.

No, no, no, no. Not yet. Not now.

Mommy, what's happening? I'm getting squeezed. I don't like this.

Its ok Alex, it will be ok.

No it won't Mommy, they're going to take me away now aren't they?! I don't want to GO Mommy!

She could hear her son start to cry. His sobs echoed through her head.

Tears ran down her face, but she tried to discreetly wipe them away. She knew they were watching, waiting. She would try to delay as long as she could.

Unfortunately, just then an excruciating pain ripped through her abdomen and a high squeal escaped through her clenched teeth. Her fists curled up until they were white. Within moments, her alien guard appeared in her room.

"*No!*" she screamed as she scrambled back into the furthest corner. "No! Nothing is happening. I'm fine. I…"

It's too soon, too soon. Not yet.

Another contraction felt like it was ripping her apart and this time she was unable to hold back. She screamed until her face was a dark red and she thought she'd pass out from lack of oxygen. When it was over, she realized she was in the hall, being carried.

She struggled, kicked and screamed until the alien dropped her. She landed with a shriek of pain, which added to the almost unbearable agony that twisted through the rest of her body.

Then her water broke and gushed across the steel floor.

Shit!

All the while she heard her sons' screams.

Mommy, no, please. Mommy, it hurts! Make it stop!

"It's too early, only eight months, can't be happening yet…" she muttered between contractions, nearly incoherent as she was picked back up.

She thought she heard the alien say "Eight months is the standard pregnancy term for our females…"

"I'm not one of *your female*s!" she screamed.

Her mind was a jumble of her own thoughts and those of her terrified child.

She dimly recognized they'd made it to another steel room, occupied by three more of the aliens. She was placed in a chair with stirrups.

One of them tried to place an I.V. in her arm but she grabbed the needle and flung in in its face. Within moments, straps appeared for the second time since she'd been here.

"Fuck you. Fuck you. Fuck you," she grated out like a mantra as she struggled against the straps being placed.

This took a while because she was beyond pain, beyond caring and the hormones coursing through her body gave her a primal strength.

"Please remain calm," one of them said.

"FUCK YOU!" she screamed, as another contraction wracked her body.

This time, the pain wrapped around to her back and clamped down on her entire middle section like a vice. She barely registered the prick of a needle in her arm. She tried to jerk her arm back, only to realize both her arms were now tied down.

As she grunted through the rest of the contraction, the pain began to lessen. It was just enough for her son's distressed wailing to rise back to her consciousness.

She grit her teeth as the taste of salt flooded her mouth. As the pain continued to recede, she began to sob as she listened to his cries.

Then she felt the overwhelming urge to push, so she did. And pushed again. Her world narrowed down to *pushing* and *not pushing*.

She wasn't sure how long it lasted - hours or minutes she couldn't say. Time had no meaning.

She screamed as she felt like her whole bottom half was going to fall off, be ripped apart, or squeeze out all of her insides. An indistinct screaming that wasn't coming from her, formed the periphery of her thoughts.

Then, Alex slid out so quickly it took her a moment to realize she'd just given birth.

"Give me my baby!" she shrieked. "Untie me right now!"

She flailed wildly against the restraints. They wrapped him up so quickly she didn't even see it happen.

"Just let me hold him! LET ME HOLD HIM!"

She strained against the straps with every fiber of her being. She thrashed and kicked out with her feet, which were still not tied down, and managed to kick a tray out of the grasp of the one coming towards her.

The alien bent over, picked up a needle, moved to her I.V. and poked it into the port. She caught a glimpse of her bawling son, just the top of his head, as he was carried out of the room.

"ALEX!"

Jess rocked the chair she was strapped to, pulled on the straps.

"Alex! Alex! Give me my baby!" she screeched.

As the door hissed shut, she thought she heard a distant wailing. She wasn't sure if it was in her head or not.

One of the aliens pulled out the stun gun she hadn't seen in months.

Jess shook her head vehemently.

"No, you can't do this. It's not right! I want my baby!" she cried.

She thought she saw regret in its eyes. *The father, then, maybe…*

He pointed the gun at her.

"Wait!" she shouted. "Wait."

He lowered the gun slightly.

"His name is Alex. Remember that, ok? Just remember, his name is Alex…his name is Alex…Remember!" she babbled. "Tell him I wanted him. Tell him… I love him…" she trailed off. She didn't know what else to say.

He gave the barest hint of a nod. At least she thought he did.

"I'm sorry," he told her. Then he raised the gun again and shot her.

She collapsed onto the chair.

Jess stared at the ceiling until whatever sedative they put into her I.V. circulated through her veins.

Then she saw nothing.

CHAPTER FIFTEEN

Jess rolled over to slap her alarm clock.

"Ughhh," she moaned.

*Why did I ask for an extra shift? They're always brutal. I only got…*she sat up to look at the clock and then threw herself back down onto her pillows…*five hours of sleep.*

She stumbled her way into the bathroom and gave herself a hard stare in the tiny cabinet mirror over the sink.

Guess you shouldn't have gone out after a twelve hour shift, when you had the morning shift today. You're not getting any younger Jess, that's for sure. Might want to reevaluate these Monday Girl's Nights.

She stuck her tongue out at her reflection.

Screw you too! she thought cheerfully and hopped in the shower. *There's no way I'm giving up Girl's Night.*

As she finished getting ready and was about to head out the door, she got the overwhelming sensation she was forgetting something.

She looked around her small apartment, trying to jump start her brain to figure out what she was missing.

She went over to the mirror hanging over the entry table and smiled to check for lipstick on her teeth.

Nope.

She sniffed her armpits to make sure she'd put on deodorant.

Yep.

She held up her purse, placed it on her entry table to rifle through it and then zipped it back up.

Well, I've got everything, far as I can tell. I'm sure I'll find out what it is, later. When it's most inconvenient.

She shrugged and sauntered out of her apartment, locked the door, and galloped down the stairs. Her super was coming up the stairs as she descended.

"Hey Walt! How are you doing this fine morning?" she chirped.

The man was hauling a huge bag up the stairs, huffing.

"Good morning Jess. I've been better, lemme tell ya. The A.C. went out in 5C, Ms. Harrington is on my ass about her damned leaky faucet again and 2B wants me to rekey their lock *for the third time*. Do you people appreciate me at all, I wonder? All I ever hear are complaints. Makes me wonder why I ever took this job…"

"I do Walt! My A.C. is working just fine." Jess winked at the grumpy old man.

"Humph," he grunted. "That's probably only because you never need me. You must have gotten the best apartment in this whole damned building."

"Well, lucky me then, I guess. Gotta go Walt. Good luck!"

The sweltering heat of summer in the city rushed in at her as she opened the door onto the street.

"Pshew!" she commented, and held the door open for her neighbors.

"Hey Jess. You gonna be around for tonight's barbeque? We're having chicken and burgers…" offered the woman, one half of a couple about her age.

"Mmm…thank you Liza, but I think I'm gonna sit this one out. I pulled a double shift yesterday and 'Girl's Night' seems to be taking more of a toll on me than usual."

She made a face.

"Getting old…"

Liza laughed.

"Right, Jess. What are you, twenty five? You can't be older than Jeremy here," she elbowed her partner, "and he's only *thirty*."

Liza rolled her eyes and it was Jess' turn to laugh.

"Well a lady never reveals her age, but since I'm not a lady, I'll be twenty seven this September. This last year has just flown!"

"Nice. I'll be twenty *eight* in November," she said in a dramatic whisper. "So, are you throwing a bash like last year?"

Jess made an exaggerated face of contemplation and tapped her finger on her chin.

"Hmm, maybe. You gonna buy me something good?"

"Oh please, like you don't already get all the best goodies from work. Lucky!"

"This is true, I am. I do enjoy my job. Well, most of the time. Speaking of, if I want to keep said job, I'd better get going. Sorry to miss your Q, Liza, Jeremy. See you guys later!"

The rest of the week passed without incident. The rounds of job, going out, socializing and her weekly phone call with her parents went off without a hitch. Then two weeks.

It was a month later that she started having inexplicable nightmares.

After waking up soaked and screaming for a week straight, she told her parents about the dreams.

"What are the dreams about?" her mother asked over the phone.

"Well, I can't really remember Ma, by the time I'm fully awake they're just gone. But I feel...horrible. Absolutely horrible. It's the strangest thing. You know I've never had a problem like this before."

Her mother's hum skittered into her ear.

"No, you haven't. How's your job going? Are you stressed out? Sleeping enough?"

"Yeah. Well – I *was* sleeping fine until I started having these damn nightmares."

"Watch your language dear."

"Mom...."

"I'm still your mother."

Jess sighed.

"Yes I am aware, Mom. But anyway, I was sleeping just fine, then *boom*, out of nowhere, I start having these crazy dreams. I'm getting a little worried. I'm...now I'm waking up way before my alarm goes off, completely soaked, and sometimes I'm even, like, screaming. It's so bizarre."

Her mother hummed again.

"That sounds serious Jess. Maybe you should go a psychologist. I can't see why you would suddenly be having nightmares, but I'm not a psychologist either. Are you sure you're alright? Has anything…happened recently?"

"No, that's what so weird about it. Nothing has happened at all. Except the dreams themselves."

"Maybe your psychologist can prescribe you something to help you sleep better."

"Psychologists don't do that here Ma."

"Well, whatever. See a psychiatrist then."

She could almost see her mother waving her hand nonchalantly in the air.

"Do you think it's serious enough for that?"

"I couldn't tell you that dear, only a doctor can."

"Right," she said in a clipped tone.

"Don't get an attitude with me missy, I'm just trying to help."

Jess sighed again.

"I know it's just…I wonder if I'm overreacting."

"One way to find out darling."

"Yeaahh," she breathed. "Let me talk to Dad."

"He's on the line," her mother confessed.

"Mom!"

"Hey sweetie," her Dad interjected. "I heard you're having some pretty bad nightmares. How you holding up?"

Jess counted to ten for patience before she answered.

"Well, if you were listening Dad, you already know."

"Humor your Pop."

She rubbed the bridge of her nose.

"I'm fine I guess. What do you think, should I go see a psychologist? Psychiatrist, whatever."

There was a pause as he considered.

"I think it couldn't hurt, sweetie. I'd rather you be taken care of over there, then deal with this all by yourself. How about this, I'll call on one of my credit cards, put you on the account, and have them issue you a card. Then if you keep having the nightmares over the next week, you can call and get yourself right in to see someone about it. Deal? That way, you have no excuse to not take care of yourself."

"Dad, I couldn't…"

"Nonsense, I won't hear any backtalk on this Jess. Clear?"

She considered her options. Not like she had many.

She thought back to this morning, the feeling of helplessness, horror and anxiety she'd felt when she woke up. She might not be able to remember the dreams, but she did know what was going on wasn't normal.

"Deal Pop."

"Good! Now let's get off the phone so I can call."

"Alright Pop, love to you and Mom."

"We love *you* Jess. We'll figure this out. Just keep us up to date would ya? If something happens between now and next week, don't wait til the normal time to call us, ok?"

"Ok Pop, you know I will. Love you guys."

"Love you too sweetie."

CHAPTER SIXTEEN

The next week went much like the last.

Jess woke up every morning drenched, disturbed and screaming. On top of that though, she also started having hallucinations. Now she was seriously freaked out.

The first couple times it happened, she thought she heard a voice calling to her, but when she turned around no one was there. It had happened first at work and she had played it off as some kids pulling a prank or just a trick of her ears or…something.

Then it happened when she was at home, which really scared her because she lived alone.

Then it happened again, and again. It ranged from saying things like; *where are you, are you ok, I miss you, I love you* - to crying and overwhelming sadness.

She was overwhelmed alright, she was turning into a walking train wreck.

By Friday she was afraid to go to sleep or be alone, but she also didn't want anyone to see her this way.

Paranoid, anxious and jumpy, she tried to shut it out. Ignore it. And it worked. Sometimes.

The night before her regular Sunday phone call with her parents, she called them. After five rings, the answering machine picked up. She left a brief message and hung up.

Dammit. Now what?

She had already passed up on going out with a group of friends, to stay at home instead. Her friend Bethany had teased her about how she must have found a new man-toy and Jess had played along. Bethany didn't want to hear about what was going wrong with her. None of her friends probably did. They weren't exactly known for their compassion and were more interested in who was dating who and partying than they were in deep, complicated emotional issues. She hadn't been any different herself before all this started happening. And furthermore she refused to be the friend who just bummed everyone else out.

Jess puttered around her apartment, cleaned up a little and then finally settled down to watch some T.V. She flicked through the menu, something she almost never did as she wasn't usually at home long enough to watch anything. She found something to watch, a nice comedy, and snuggled down into her couch.

She enjoyed the show for about an hour, before the faint voice in her mind became too distracting.

*I love you....come back....*and then chattering on about complete nonsense.

She turned the T.V. volume up and focused intensely on the show. After another half hour, it became entirely unenjoyable due to the level of concentration she was exerting.

She flung the remote down onto the cushions and stomped over to her freezer, pulled out a bottle of vanilla vodka she kept stashed and rummaged around for a shot glass.

If I can't even watch T.V. in peace, I'll just drown out the voice.

She downed two shots then headed to the living room with the bottle.

Six shots and an hour later, she wasn't even sure what she was watching anymore. She was concentrating so hard, yet at the same time couldn't describe the show she was watching if her life depended on it.

She slammed back two more shots, turned off the T.V. and headed to her bedroom. She connected her phone to a

Bluetooth speaker, selected a playlist and turned the volume up, then plopped onto her bed with a loud sigh.

The alcohol didn't work, the music didn't work. Distraction didn't work.

What the hell is happening to me?

She could still hear the voice.

Maybe it will stop if I talk back to it? At this point, I don't care if it's crazy or not. I just want it to go away.

So she gave it a try.

Hello? She said to it tentatively.

Mommy? Oh Mommy, I miss you so much! I was so worried about you.

Why the hell are you calling me Mommy? What kind of sick part of myself are you?

Mommy, what's wrong?

I'm not your 'Mommy', stop calling me that ok?!

Don't you love me anymore Mommy? Why not? It's not my fault they made you go away! I know it's not your fault either. We tried everything...

She flung herself out of the bed.

No. Ok, clearly that was a bad idea.

She got her vodka back out of the freezer and took two more shots.

Then she padded back to her bed, turned the music up louder still and tried to block the voice with everything she had. Eventually, she managed to fall asleep.

She woke up screaming and covered in a slick layer of sweat. The bile rising in her throat created an acidic burning sensation and she swallowed several times to force it back into her stomach. She couldn't remember a damn thing about the dream, but her whole body was shaking and she was inexplicably terrified.

She looked at the clock, 6 a.m. She clutched her head as sharp pain shot through her skull and laid back down with a groan.

There is no way I'm going to be able to make it into work today. Not sure why I thought drinking so much would be a good idea.

She snorted.

Oh right, I'm hearing an effing voice in my head…

She waited until an hour before her shift was supposed to start and left a voice mail for her boss.

Then she called her parents again. She told them about the voice. A long silence descended over the line while her mother processed the latest news.

"My goodness dear, is there anywhere you can get into today? It doesn't sound like this is something that can wait."

'Yeah I'm sure there is…but Mom, Dad - is there any history of anything like this in the family? I just don't understand how something like this can be happening to me, out of the blue."

"Hmm, well my great Uncle Gene had hypoglycemia but other than that…" Her mother trailed off.

"My Grandfather had hand tremors when he was older, but his doctor said it was a side effect of one of his medications." Her father interjected.

"So that would be a no."

"No dear, I'm afraid not. At least it's not in your family history," her mother said.

"Are you sure you're not just really stressed out sweetie? I know how horrible that city can be for a person. Maybe you should consider moving back home. You could stay with us for a while."

She stifled a laugh at her father's transparent overprotective streak.

"Thanks Dad, but this is where I want to be. We've gone over this."

"I know, I know. Just putting it on there, so you know you're welcome at any time Jess. It's an option."

She smiled.

"Thanks Pop."

"Anytime kiddo."

She could hear the smile in her father's voice. She sighed.

"Well, I guess I should get off the phone and call around."

"You do that dear, and call us right away after your appointment."

"Ok Ma. Talk to you in a bit."

CHAPTER SEVENTEEN

Jess walked out onto the street, clutching the paper bag holding her new prescription.

She thought the appointment had gone well. Dr. Itzkoff hadn't wanted to just throw medication at her and had seemed to genuinely listen to her and take her seriously. She hadn't felt ignored or that he was condescending or dismissive.

He had prescribed her some Valium for the anxiety and for its sedative properties to help her sleep, and told her to come back in three days. He had also suggested she try communicating with the voice as a way of lessening its disturbing projection into her consciousness.

She still wasn't sure that was a good idea, but decided to at least consider trying it again.

He had been baffled at first by her assertion that she hadn't experienced any emotional trauma, as hearing voices was usually a result of a traumatic experience. But it seemed like he believed her.

She pulled out the bottled water she'd pilfered from the doctor's office, unscrewed the bottle of pills and took one. By the time she got home, it started to take effect and she stumbled her way into her apartment.

Her bed called to her from the living room, so she trudged into her bedroom and landed on the bed with a solid thump. Within minutes she was out.

When she woke up, after a blissfully dreamless sleep, it was almost midnight.

The Voice, as she'd started to think of it - as a distinct personality - immediately started in.

Mommy, are you ok? What is happening to you?

She groaned.

God, not again. Why the hell am I going so totally crazy?

You're not crazy Mommy, you just can't remember me.

A chill ran down her spine.

This is waaay too creepy.

But she recalled the doctor's advice.

Listen, I don't know why you think I'm your 'Mommy' but you've got to stop this ok? You're really messing up my life here. I mean, maybe in a manner of speaking I am your

'Mommy', since you only exist in my head. But I don't want you here! I've got a life to live and you're cramping my style.

A wave of incredible sadness washed over her.

Why don't you love me anymore Mommy?

Listen Voice, I'm not your Mommy and I don't know why you think I should love you!

There was a long silence.

Thank god.

She got up and went to go take another pill. As she opened the cap, The Voice intruded again so suddenly she jerked in surprise and the pills went flying all over her kitchen floor.

"God-*dammit*!" she yelped.

She slammed the nearly empty bottle onto the counter and bent over to pick up the scattered pills.

Mommy, it's ok if you don't remember me. They told me they erased your memories. But you will remember me one day. I still love you, no matter what. I am not 'Voice', I am Alex. That's the name you *gave me. You will remember eventu-*

Jesus Christ, would you just shut up!

Another surge of sadness, and then silence.

She tried to ignore the strange feeling she got as she recognized the name Alex, from one of her best friends from school.

But of course it would know about Alex, this Voice is coming from my own mind.

Within a few minutes, it was back

I'll leave you alone now Mommy, I remember what you taught me about separate spaces. I will talk to you later.

She waited for a few long, drawn out moments, waiting for it to come back. When it didn't, she was nothing but relieved.

Phew. Maybe the doctor is right, talking to it seems to help. Huh.

She wandered over to her T.V. and sat down to watch something while she waited for the pill to kick in.

True to its 'word', the Voice didn't disturb her for several hours, though she occasionally heard distant things going on, almost like background noise. Finally, she couldn't keep her eyes open any longer and went to bed as the sun rose.

She woke up at about noon - drenched again, screaming and crying.

For the life of her, she couldn't remember what the dream had been about though. Aside from the fact she felt like she was going to crawl out of her own skin, she couldn't pinpoint what was actually *wrong*.

Her heart raced and she reached out a shaking hand for the glass of water on her bedside table. Then she squeezed her eyes shut and took some deep breaths to slow her heartrate. With a sigh, she got out of bed and went to the kitchen to take another pill.

Well, apparently this is just my life now. Guess I'd better get used to it.

Today was a day off for her, so she decided she'd had about enough of moping around her apartment. She would go for a nice walk to the park, maybe do some shopping and have lunch with Bethany and Alicia.

There's no point in becoming a total shut in. I've got to try to keep my shit together here.

She texted the girls and hopped into the shower.

By the time she was done, both of them had replied enthusiastically about lunch. So she finished getting ready and headed out for her walk.

Lunch went well, both the girls teased her about her mysterious lover and she laughed and played along. She still wasn't willing to tell her friends just how sideways her life was sliding.

The Valium made her a more than a bit sluggish, but she found she was able to overcome this by guzzling multiple double shot lattes.

Huh. I might be able to make this work after all.

Over the next couple of weeks, Jess tried to adjust to her new experience. The Voice receded a bit, though the nightmares continued unabated. In fact, they seemed to be getting slightly worse as time went on.

She started avoiding taking the Valium because it made her sleepy, and became very familiar with late night infomercials.

After a several more visits with Dr. Itzkoff, he started gently mentioning the possibility of her taking an antipsychotic drug for the Voice. He also suggested a sleep study. She wasn't sure she was ready to do a sleep study, but she kept it on the back burner in her thoughts. Maybe it could help…

She managed to wade through the next month after that, but her boss was losing patience with her lateness, her sluggish performance, and the increased amount of days she called in sick.

By the time Thanksgiving rolled around and her parents flew in for a visit, Jess was struggling to function at a normal level. She still heard The Voice and now she'd begun getting these strange…visions, for lack of a better word. Hallucinations?

She'd been embarrassed to admit it, even to Dr. Itzkoff, but she had begun seeing flashes of a massive kidnapping operation, where she was one of hundreds of victims. Fantastical and horrifying scenes of being chased and restrained, drugged and paralyzed.

She'd begun finding it harder and harder to leave her apartment at all. She knew it wasn't real and that she had no cause to be afraid, but she couldn't seem to convince her body of that fact.

When the visions hit, she froze. She couldn't speak or think, all her muscles went rigid and she could hardly breathe. Several times, she barely avoided calling an ambulance, when she was almost convinced she was having a heart attack.

It was insane. She *felt* insane.

The doctor was still trying to not so subtly push her for details on the traumatic event she'd experienced that was behind all this, but there just…wasn't one.

She didn't know why any of this was happening. It seemed like one day she woke up and her mind had decided to snap.

At her parent's urging, she agreed to start taking an antipsychotic and switched to a long term antianxiety medication.

Neither helped.

The Voice continued to talk to her. While it was generally pleasant to talk to, despite the disturbing tendency of it calling her 'Mommy', the visual hallucinations pushed her over the edge.

One night, under a relentless onslaught of unbearable visions where she was being held captive, combined with constant chatter and noise from the Voice, she accidentally overdosed.

The combination of antipsychotic and antianxiety medications along with the alcohol she knew she wasn't supposed to drink, but had anyways in a fit of desperation - put her into a coma.

CHAPTER EIGHTEEN

A middle aged, female doctor strode down the hall towards Jess' parents, who were seated in the hospital waiting room. The woman stretched out her hand to them as she approached and introduced herself.

"Mr. and Mrs. Richards, I'm Dr. Suresh."

"How's she doing?" Jess' father asked anxiously.

Dr. Suresh flipped open the metal chart she was holding and studied it silently for several moments.

"We went ahead and give Jess a CT scan and a MRI as well as a complete blood panel, to see if we could find any physiological causes for her sudden presentation of mental illness."

She flipped another page on the chart.

"Both scans came back perfectly normal, there are no tumors or physical abnormalities to speak of. However, the presence of a qualifying biomarker in her blood panel flagged her for inclusion in an experimental study we're running with the National Institute of Health. And that *did* turn up an interesting result. We ran Jess' results through a specialized analysis software we're testing as part of the study. Th-"

"Is she still in the coma?"

"No. She recovered from the coma last night. However, when she woke up she was in a state of extreme agitation and we were concerned about her hurting herself or our staff, so she is now heavily sedated. That is what led us to conduct the scans actually - which were completed while she was under sedation."

"Oh my god, what did she do?" her mother asked.

Dr. Suresh lowered the chart.

"The nurses told me she seemed to believe she was being…abducted by aliens. She actually struck our most senior nurse and fled down the hallway. By the time she was apprehended, she was incoherent - screaming and crying about aliens. We're not sure she realized where she was."

"Oh my god," Ms. Richards repeated and a hand flew up to cover her mouth in disbelief.

"Don't worry, the situation is under control and she is now resting peacefully. Our staff is quite used to…rough behavior from patients, let's just say."

She picked up the chart again and turned a few pages.

"As I was saying before, the results of the analysis from the molecular biology lab indicated that Jess has a peculiar epistasis of the epithalamus, which has led to unstable protein regulation and the corruption of portions of her mitochondrial DNA."

Jess' father spoke up.

"I'm sorry doctor, can you dumb it down for us a little? What does that mean in layman's terms?

"In short it means that it's likely a genetic mutation has occurred in Jess' brain, which is superimposing incorrect functioning over her previous gene expression. This would explain, at least partially, her hallucinations. The role of the epithalamus is connected to the pineal gland, which as far as we know dictates the hormonal responses related to the production of melatonin. You may be familiar with this as an over the counter sleep aid, but sleep regulation is only one of the functions of the hormone."

Both of Jess' parents gave the doctor blank stares.

Dr. Suresh tried again.

"If this is the abnormality causing or contributing to Jess' parasomnia - her nightmares - the resultant lack of quality sleep from continually disturbed REM cycles, *can* cause hallucinations. As far as the rest of it, the science is still unclear or ill defined."

"So you're saying a lack of sleep because of a gene…problem, could be causing the hallucinations? But then why did she start experiencing the nightmares in the first place?" Mrs. Richards asked.

"Honestly, we're not sure. The best evidence we have for the change is this mutation. Melatonin is also thought to be involved in protecting against neurodegeneration, so if Jess is experiencing deregulation of this hormone, degeneration may account for some of her central nervous system symptoms, the anxiety and then the panic disorder. It may play a part in the hallucinations as well."

"So what is the plan, er - prognosis?" Jess' father asked.

"Short of exploratory brain surgery, there is not much we can do to more fully diagnose her with - or treat her for - anything more specific than schizophrenia with paranoia and parasomnia. I could potentially recommend some kind of gene therapy, but we can't classify the genetic material that's causing the mutation. It's not any identifiable disease that our existing knowledge of medical science can treat."

Both of Jess' parents jaws dropped open and they stared at the doctor uncomprehendingly.

"I would say this all presents as a very severe case of Post-Traumatic Stress Disorder, aside from the issues that could arise from the disruption of sleep patterns. But according to Jess, she hasn't suffered any kind of triggering event. Can you tell me anything she might be hesitant to share with our staff? Her concern about aliens during this last episode gives us further reason to believe this is trauma based. An 'alien' could be a stand in fantasy figure her mind has created in replacement of a person she has encountered, and been traumatized by. I spoke with her psychiatrist, Dr. Itzkoff, and he concurred, though he told me Jess hadn't yet shared the traumatizing event with him."

Jess' mother shook her head slowly, still dazed by the baffling flow of information.

"No, not that we're aware of doctor, and she would have told us herself if something had happened. I'm sure you hear this all the time from parents, but we're very close. She tells us practically everything. What about this…genetic mutation? How does something like that happen? Is this something she inherited from us?"

"In this case - no. This doesn't appear to be an inherited disease, as there is no history of mental disease in either of your families and she had none of the early indicators. A genetic mutation can occur spontaneously. Or it can be caused through exposure to certain chemicals or radiation, even cell migration if she's had a child. Have any of these scenarios occurred with Jess? We attempted to ask *her* this same question before the sedatives took full effect, but her current level of distress suggested it would be a good idea to double check with family members that might be informed on her medical history."

"Exposure to chemicals or radiation…no I can't see why she would. She works in retail!"

"Did she sustain a pregnancy, for any length of time, that we're not aware of?"

Jess' mother snorted.

"Certainly not. She's not exactly interested in children, she's on birth control."

"Is it possible she had an abortion? And maybe experienced emotional trauma because of it? Did you know that 77% of cases presenting with her symptoms are the result of a traumatic experience?"

"What? No, definitely not." She waved her hand in the air dismissively.

Dr. Suresh gave them both a hard look.

"Are you sure?"

"Very. We talk to her every week and visit a few times a year. We were just here for the Fourth of July! She shares everything with us. We would have known."

"What about drugs or alcohol? Has she ever had any substance abuse issues?"

Her mother snorted again.

"Jess? No, she has never had a drug problem and she did drink a little too much for our liking, but she's not an alcoholic. Believe me, we would have been all over her if she was, made her go to rehab and AA."

The doctor hummed but let it drop.

"Then I can only assume this was a spontaneous mutation. If fetomaternal microchimerism were indicated we could do more testing to determine that. Not that it would do much aside from give us more information. There's not much to be done if it were."

"Fetal…micro…what? What are you saying doctor?"

"The bottom line here is - there is little we can do for Jess but keep her well medicated and under observation. Unless you want her to participate in what would probably end up being a lifetime of clinical studies and trials, to try to figure out a way to treat her unique condition."

"Goodness."

Jess' mother plopped down onto the chair in the waiting room. Mr. Richards turned to place a hand on her shoulder.

"We can admit her to the best psychiatric hospital available, where she'll be well cared for. Provided, of course, you or your insurance company is willing to cover her admission and inpatient costs. You'll need to speak with the hospital's admission manager about the details. I'm going to refer her to the local hospital, it's one of the best and biggest in the country. We can reevaluate her treatment protocols at any time you or she deems fit. I'd also like to submit her to the study they're conducting on schizophrenia if you-"

Her father turned back to the doctor.

"No doctor, we're going to decline on that, thank you. Jess wouldn't like that, she wouldn't want that. Especially in light of her recent episodes. I think peace and quiet would benefit her more."

"Are you sure, the studies could-"

"We're sure doctor, thank you."

"Ok. Here's my card if you need anything else or come up with any more questions."

She pulled a card out of one of her deep lab coat pockets, flipped it over and scribbled on the back.

"And here's the number for the admissions manager for the psychiatric hospital. Good luck to you both, and to Jess. I think, in time, she will recover from this. Many people with schizophrenia lead perfectly normal lives. After the three day observation period, we'll go ahead and transfer her over, if she consents. If she doesn't, you can start the involuntary admission process if you like."

"Thank you doctor." Mr. Richards replied.

Dr. Suresh turned and walked back down the hallway.

Jess' parents just looked at each, shock and bewilderment etched deeply into their faces.

CHAPTER NINETEEN

Jess watched as snow floated down to the river, stories below, and dissolve as it landed on the water. She heard a group of interns coming down the hallway through her open door.

Ugh, here they come to gawk again. Maybe I should have listened to Mom and Dad about finding a hospital outside of the city after all.

Its ok Mommy, they don't stay long.

She sighed.

I know Alex, it's just…irritating.

It had taken a year, but Jess had come to terms with the Voice. She had learned as much as she could about schizophrenia and had stopped trying to suppress it – him, whatever. While she still had a certain level of distaste towards it calling her Mommy, she couldn't dissuade him from calling her that no matter how hard she tried. So she had given up on it a couple months ago.

Dr. Itzkoff had contracted with the hospital for courtesy privileges and was still managing her care, along with Dr. Suresh. She had a protocol management session with Dr. Suresh every quarter and both her doctors seemed to be pretty cooperative with each other. They were good doctors and she considered herself lucky to have them in charge of her treatment.

They didn't rush her, didn't make her go *too* far out of her comfort zone, which she appreciated. She wasn't sure she was ready for the dive into outpatient care. When her panic attacks hit…

She understood she blacked out, because it had been explained to her several times. She still struggled to really comprehend the scope of her illness because she could remember so little of her worst episodes. The dreams, the 'states of extreme agitation and delirium' as Dr. Suresh called them, it was hard to believe they really happened to *her*, because she couldn't remember them.

Remember I told you, they aren't panic attacks Mommy, they are memories. *You are so special they couldn't even completely erase your memories of me. Because you love me so much.*

She felt a little mental hug and smiled.

Alex, we've talked about this and you know what Dr. Itzkoff says.

Well, he's wrong you know. You're wrong too. I am not a delusion, I'm real. I'm a person. You'll see one day.

She shook her head and tried to pick back up on her previous train of thought.

She had tried to get a definitive answer on how long she might need to be here, but Dr. Itzkoff had thus far only given her the answer of "you'll know when you're ready to take the leap of faith back into the world, Jess" and smiled at her.

Whatever the hell that was supposed to mean.

She had overheard him and Dr. Suresh discussing her care one day about a month ago, a little ways down the hallway outside her room. She recalled the conversation quite well.

You know we're not going to be able to release her until she regains some control over these violent delirious episodes. Dr. Suresh had said. *If she ever does. Or we at least get a handle on her triggers, which are still entirely unpredictable.*

I know. Dr. Itzkoff replied. *No matter how deep I try to dig with her, I can't seem to uncover the underlying cause of her trauma. She's got to have one. It's the only reasonable, or medical, explanation for the presentation of her symptoms. It's like she's...completely blocked it. I've seen a few cases like this before, but this is the most severe I've ever dealt with. Even with the medications, I'm not sure we'll ever make substantial progress. Whatever happened to her, it was bad. So bad her brain has quarantined it to a place I don't know how to access.*

Well her parents certainly aren't helping with that. They continue to insist nothing happened, even though they live hundreds of miles away...

At that point they had moved down the hallway until she couldn't hear them anymore.

Despite the conversation between her doctors she still held on to the belief that she could, one day *soon*, resume her normal life.

Her parents were subletting her apartment, so it would be ready and waiting for her when she was ready to leave the hospital. She supposed she could find another job in retail or something.

If the medication she was on continued to provide the same promising results. If she could get ahead of the blackouts…

Within six months, they'd managed to find a combination of medications that reduced the terrifying hallucinations to a manageable level. She still had the nightmares a couple times a week and went through extended periods of insomnia. Though the frequency had diminished to about twice a month, she continued to have the episodes and both doctors insisted she stay in hospital for round the clock observation and access to trained staff. So for the time being, she was content enough with her arrangement.

I never thought I'd say it, but Alex has been the one thing holding me together. He seems to calm me down when nothing else can.

Thank you Mommy! the Voice chimed in again. *I want to help you. You're very sad. It makes me sad too. No one here talks about feelings like you do. My father is the only one who lets me talk about them sometimes. But he doesn't really like when I do. I can tell, I can feel it. I can talk to him in his head too, you know.*

She smiled and shook her head again. Quite an elaborate personality she'd created.

In her twice weekly group therapy sessions, she had realized she was actually very lucky with her Voice.

Alex always said he loved her, and tried to take care of her in his way. Some of her group dealt with nasty, insulting, derogatory voices and Alex would never say anything like that to her.

She almost felt smug sometimes.

Alex and I have a relationship that I wouldn't call healthy per se, but at least it's not as downright unhealthy as some of the people in group.

Like that one girl, Cathy. She was always talking about how Satan is real and lives in a spaceship far away and that he takes women to space and makes them have babies and then sends them back. And she was going to find a way to go back and find her baby.

She shuddered.

It could always be worse…

EPILOGUE

30 Years Later

Jess Richards pushed her ancient shopping cart down the alley at a snail's pace. A cold wind gusted down the narrow passage and she stopped to pull the tattered collar of her moth-eaten wool men's overcoat up around her neck. She'd considered it excellent luck to have found it in the dumpster just in time for the cold weather.

Last year had been the hardest yet, in the four since both of her parents died. Her mother had gone five years ago, her father the year after.

Within a month of her father's death, she had been discharged her from the hospital she'd called home for the previous twenty six years, give or take.

Her parents had died essentially penniless from almost three decades of top-notch inpatient care for her. When the money for her care stopped flowing in, she had been unceremoniously deemed 'not a threat to self or others' and they had called her a cab.

Since she had nowhere to go, she'd hopped right out of the cab and wandered around the city carrying the small knapsack that contained all the pieces of her life in the hospital. It was very light.

She could still remember several attempts, in the early days, at conditional release from the hospital. The first time she'd only made it a week before the first blackout episode that landed her back in the E.R. She had assaulted a handful of police officers and only narrowly avoided being charged thanks to Dr. Suresh vouching for her. At least that's what she's been told.

Other attempts over the years had provided similar results until her doctors had essentially given up on the idea of outpatient care.

Now she just avoided being around people at all, so that when she had the episodes, she couldn't get into trouble.

Jess shook her head.

Was I ever really that young? It feels like too many lifetimes ago...

Of course you were Mom, I remember how brave you were. You still are.

Flattery will get you everywhere, Alex.

I won't have to flatter you at all soon, Mom. I am close to you now.

Ok Alex, ok.

She looked around in the dark alley for a good spot to nestle down for the night.

Not too bad. There's light at the end of the alley, but it's not hitting me in the face when I lay down behind this dumpster here.

Oh Mom, I'm so sorry it's taken me so long to get to you. I'll make it up to you, I promise.

No worries Alex, she thought with a sigh.

The Voice had been telling her for the last couple months that he was 'coming for her' to 'take care of her'. She fully understood this was just wishful thinking feeding her delusional companion.

She burrowed down into the nest of relatively clean newspaper she had acquired in the city throughout the day as she meandered her way up and down the streets.

As she had gotten older, she'd found it a little bit easier to fall asleep, though she still struggled with recurrent insomnia and of course, the nightmares she couldn't remember.

After about an hour of listening to the constant, restless sounds of the city, she fell asleep. An indeterminate amount of time later, she was awoken by repetitious shouts.

God, now what? If any of these street hooligans try to mess with me again, I'll be happy to give them another face full of my trusty pepper spray. Just like the one last week learned firsthand...

Mom!

Oh, Alex. Alex! Why on Earth did you wake me up? I'm old as shit, I need my rest bucko.

"Mom!" she heard again, only it sounded like it came from the end of the alley.

That's impossible.

"Not impossible, Mom. I'm here. Just like I said I would be."

"Oh my god, this is a whole new level of crazy," she muttered as she scrambled out of her newspaper nest and peeked around the dumpster.

She nearly fell over when she saw a figure at the end of the alley, under the light. It wore a long, hooded coat but she couldn't make out any other details.

"There is no effing way. Apparently now I have dementia too," she continued to mutter as she stood up, smoothed her filthy coat and stepped out from behind the dumpster.

"Hi Mom. I finally found you."

She couldn't be sure, but she thought it looked like the person was smiling.

Jess crept cautiously toward the figure, fingering the pepper spray in her pocket. As she approached she noticed the person had a strangely shaped head. Bigger than normal, stretching back away from the forehead much more than it should have. And *tall*.

What is this deformed guy doing in my damn alley in the middle of the night?

"Hey! I'm not deformed, Mom. I'm mixed. I've told you that."

She gasped and her hand flew to her mouth.

"Oh my god," she managed through her wrinkled, age spotted fingers.

Her knees buckled and the man flew forward to catch her. As she was confronted with the physicality of the figure, she began to understand that this might *not* be another hallucination.

Her hands groped over his arms and torso to further verify he was real.

"This isn't…this can't be…*Alex??*" she ended with a hoarse whisper.

"Yep. It's me. I'm here to take you away Mom. I told you I'd take care of you."

"All these years…"

Tears welled up in her eyes.

"I've always been real Mom. I just couldn't prove it to you until now. I couldn't get away. I'm so sorry. I would have come for you years ago but they wouldn't let me."

"Wait, who wouldn't let you?

Alex sighed.

"It's a long story. But we'll have plenty of time to catch up. Things are going to be very different from here on out, I promise you that."

He grinned down at her.

"Are you ready?"

"Well…yeah…I….let me get my things…"

What am I saying, my things are all trash.

She sniffled.

I'll get you brand new things Mom.

Jess gasped.

"Its….it's really you!"

He grinned at her again.

"The one and only. C'mon, let's get out of here."

He took a step back and held out a hand to her. She placed her own shaking hand into it.

"I'm sorry, Mom," Alex said and he led her out of the alley.

Acknowledgments

I'd like to be thank my amazing husband for his unwavering support, my family for always cheering me on, and the friends who gave me great feedback; Necia, Curtis, Paulette, Rebecca, Paige, Rob, Katherine, Laurie and Tara Sue. Thank you so much guys!

And B-rad, keep being awesome.

Keep reading for a sneak preview of Livelihood, the sequel to Motherhood. Coming December 2016!

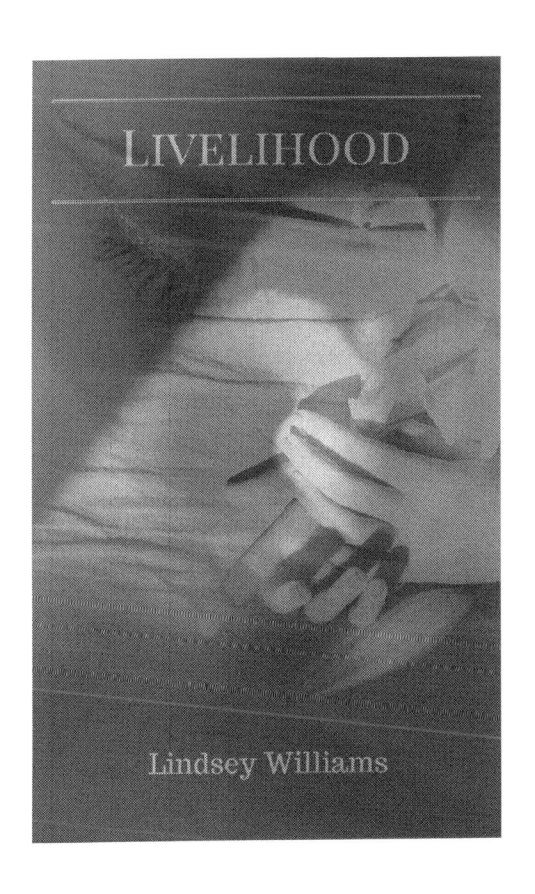

CHAPTER ONE

2045

Lily Taylor leaned forward to turn up the radio. One of her favorite songs now blasted appropriately from the speakers, as it should.

She darted a furtive glance at her Dad for his reaction.

He rolled his eyes but she saw a small smile play across his lips. He even gamely tapped his fingers on the steering wheel for her benefit.

She turned to look out the window, mostly to hide her own smile.

The song ended a few minutes later and her Dad turned down the radio with a wince as a cheesy commercial roared to life through the speakers of the SUV.

"So, pumpkin-"

Lily snorted.

"Hey, you may be seventeen now, but you'll always be my little pumpkin. I changed plenty of your poo-filled diapers, I think I've earned that right. *Anyways*, like I was gonna say, did you ever hear back from Declan on going to the movies sometime when you get back in the fall?" He wiggled his eyebrows at her hopefully.

Lily groaned.

"*Dad*, I'd rather not discuss…my love life with you on this trip, if you don't mind."

Mr. Taylor chuckled and tried to cover it up with a cough.

"There's nothing to be embarrassed about pumpkin."

"Yeah, I know. Literally, there's nothing."

"That's what worries me sweetie. You should be going out and having some fun. It's all I can do to get you out of the house for swim practice. And then you hustle it out of there as if you were being chased by a swarm of bees."

Lily sighed.

"Dad, can we…not talk about this?"

He continued on as if she hadn't spoken.

"It's just that…since your mother…passed, you haven't shown an interest in hardly anything Lily. You should be getting out there, doing stuff that teenage girls do. You know, giggling over boys and stuff!"

He looked over at her with an exaggerated, open mouthed grin.

"Dad. Seriously?" She laughed and gave him a mock warning look.

He held up a hand in surrender.

"I know, I know. I'm just saying, you should be socializing more. I bet your friends miss you."

"I'm just busy with…stuff. I want to do well next year."

It was her father's turn to snort.

"The last month of school you went to the exchange to download *all* of next year's first semester books. It was the entire reason I called this emergency road trip."

She cringed. She had suspected as much.

"And what's wrong with being academically prepared?"

"It's not that I'm against you being dedicated to your academic career Lily. You know that. You're so damn smart, I fully expect you to be the most kickass sci-tech engineer in existence. It's that I'm afraid you're using it as a cover to avoid dealing with…everything that happened in the last year."

Lily didn't need the reminder.

Her mother had been hit by a stray high velocity round from a police shooting incident seven months ago. The shot had gone wide from its intended target and caught Lerato Taylor in the temple. The bullet had torn through a couple ventricles in her brain and caused immediate and fatal hydrocephalus, according to the doctors. She'd been pronounced dead on arrival.

Tears stung Lily's eyes as she thought about her mother. They'd been close. Really close.

She loved her Dad too, of course, he was wonderful. The best Dad a girl could ask for, in fact. Strong, sensitive, supportive, open, with a great sense of humor.

But her relationship with her mother had been different, special. Unlike the relationships between some of her friends and their mothers, they had rarely fought or even bickered, seeming to understand each other on some unspoken level.

And she was gone forever.

"That's not it Dad."

She blinked rapidly to get rid of the tears before they could drop. She hated crying. She'd certainly cried enough in the last several months to last the rest of her life, as far she was concerned.

"You know the therapist told you that everyone heals on their own schedule. That's all it is. I just...I need time is all."

Her father nodded and the car fell into silence, the remote sounds of another ridiculous ad barely discernible in the background.

He tried, was trying, the poor man. She understood, really. He'd lost his wife of twenty years and his daughter had turned into a virtual recluse.

She just hadn't been able to muster up much interest in anything aside from her education. It was the one thing she could dedicate herself too. Knowledge. It didn't judge, it didn't require her to address her feelings. Or feel them. It just patiently waited for her to learn it.

It was what she needed, wanted, an escape. She avoided talking about her feelings at all cost. The loss was still too big for her to really wrap her mind around.

Now, here she was on the road, the miles flying by underneath them. She'd actually been looking forward to it. A change of scenery. She figured it would be good for her, change up her routine, let her forget for a while.. just pretend her Mom had stayed at home this time.

Until her Dad started to talk about her *feelings*.
Ugh.

She looked around for something, anything to change the subject. Skyscrapers were faintly visible on the horizon in front of them.

"Oh look! We're getting close to the city. How long, do you think?"

Her Dad glared at her from the corner of his eye.

"Please, like I don't see what you're doing."

"What? Really, I'm curious."

"Probably about ten minutes."

"Awesome," she replied shortly.

Awkward silence still reined as they reached the outskirts of the city minutes later.

He's probably trying to come up with another way to talk about Mom, she thought with another snort.

Then she noticed the smoke that was curling up into the sky around some of the buildings in the heart of the city.

"Do you see that??"

"Yeah," he father answered. "I do. I can't imagine they're having a bonfire in the middle of the city…" he trailed off.

"Should we keep going?" she asked.

"Well, our hotel is downtown and this is the quickest route. I can't see how going another way will help."

She looked over to see he was biting his lower lip.

"Do you think it will really be ok to head straight into…whatever is going on in there? We could always books another hotel somewhere else."

He stopped chewing his lip, with what looked like some effort.

"No, it should be fine. Probably just a fire in an old building or something."

"Yeah, you're probably right."

Traffic slowed to a crawl until they were surrounded on all sides by a sea of cars on the six lane highway. Over the next fifteen minutes they only traveled about half a mile. It was enough to put them in the gloom of the first skyscrapers. Along with the smoke, it made for quite a dismal view.

"Well, too late now," she quipped, trying to ease the tension she was feeling.

She couldn't put her finger on it, but *something* wasn't right about this situation. They'd run into traffic before in a couple other cities but even the traffic around Miami wasn't this bad.

"What a great road trip," she joked again, trying her best to set aside the unease building in the pit of her stomach.

Why should she be so worried about a little bit of traffic anyways? No big deal.

And smoke, she reminded herself. As if she had forgotten.

The sound of sirens began to reach them through the car. Her Dad looked in the rear view mirror, so Lily looked in the side mirror. It wasn't coming from behind them. Not like they would be able to get out of the way even if it was.

"Jeez," her Dad breathed.

"What do you think is going on?"

"Has to be an accident or something," he answered.

She just nodded and continued to dart her eyes around the road in front of them, straining to see anything though the increasing cloud of smoke, and the trucks and cars in front of them.

"Maybe something big even," he continued. He was obviously trying to distract her with an analytical discussion.

Nice try Dad.

"Yeah," she clipped.

"*Shit!*" her father yelped, as they heard rapid-fire gunshots in close range.

"Oh my god!" Lily simultaneously squealed.

"Get down! Lily, get down!"

They both wiggled frantically down in the seats, then half wedged themselves onto the floor. It was just in time to miss the bullet that shattered the windshield. They covered their heads with their arms as the glass rained down on them.

Before she could take another breath, she heard another burst of bullets. Something warm splattered across her face. She lifted her head from beneath her arms and looked over to see her father slumped into a limp ball.

The side of his face was blown half away and blood flowed steadily from the new gaping hole in his neck.

"*DAAAD!*" she screamed.

Her car door flew open and a burly, soot covered man leaned down and grabbed her by the arms. He dragged her out of the car and stood her up, then leered down at her.

The expression on his grimy face instantly turned her stomach. Without thought, she kicked him in the crotch with all her adrenaline-fueled might and he dropped like a stone.

She turned and sprinted away from him, weaving through the cars and people now fleeing in every direction on the road.

Lily risked a glance back to see the man was laboriously climbing to his feet. She turned back and pumped her legs as fast as they would go. The benefit of all that swim practice quickly showed itself, allowing her to sprint away with relative ease. After a while, she felt she was far enough away from her would-be abductor to slow down and assess the situation.

As she'd raced away from the road and further into the city to lose the creep in the mass of people, things had not improved. People were running everywhere, a thick haze of bitter smoke hung low to the ground between the tall buildings, and gunshots erupted with fair regularity around her. It was like a freaking riot.

No it is *a freaking riot.*

She grimly shook her head and continued to jog into the city. She'd find an off the beaten path alley and just hunker down until the rioting died down. Or maybe she could find her hotel. And then she would…

Well, you don't really know what the hell to do, do you Lily? You're in a city that's mid-riot, which you've never even seen before. And you're…a…a…

Even her mind didn't want to put the word together, what she'd become in a split second.

An orphan.

KEEP THE THRILL ALIVE WITH LINDSEY WILLIAMS' OTHER TITLES, AVAILABLE ON AMAZON

COMING SOON, FROM THE BRILLIANTLY TWISTED MIND OF LINDSEY WILLIAMS

ABOUT THE AUTHOR

Photo © Lindsey Williams

Lindsey Williams is an all organic, free-range human, and occasional poet turned self-published author.

She is a Jane-of-all-trades sort who is passionate about a variety of social issues. Some of her hobbies include researching and/or analyzing pretty much everything to death, conducting culinary experiments, and listening to really loud heavy metal while relaxing in her pool.

You can check out all the latest, and get in touch through her website: lindseymwilliams83.wix.com/author

Made in the USA
Columbia, SC
14 September 2019